STRONG COFFEE

For information about RLB Hartmann, visit
www.rlbhartmann.com

There you will find links, videos, book covers, biographical
tidbits, and other works by this author.

Strong Coffee

RLB Hartmann

Catawba River Press

Morganton, NC

Strong Coffee
A Runaway Road Story
This version © 2013

RLB Hartmann

ISBN-13: 978-0615736426
ISBN-10: 0615736424

Covers designed by Philip Davetas
augmented by RLB Hartmann

Episode 1

It's summer. Old Collins' idea of an end-of-school-term party is a lame picnic out by the chain link fence. The eight-year-olds are over at the sprinkler, smearing ice cream on each other's faces and washing it off in the rotating spray. The Almost Outs — five guys who are nearly 18 — sit on the picnic tables, bare feet muddying up the bench seats.

The rest of us huddle in the shade of the biggest tree, finishing the bologna sandwiches before they start to grow botulism or maggots, whichever comes first. I wasn't paying much attention in biology this semester. Steve and Jerry kept giving me grief over making A's all the time. "Why should you, Vinnie?" Jerry said once. "Who do you need to impress?" I told him, "Whoever will be reading my record when I get out of here." Here, meaning East Wind School for Boys. It sounds like a reformatory, and it's run like one, but it's really what used to be called an orphanage. We're all here because nobody wants us.

Jerry cusses, low so Collins can't hear him, because foul language earns points that get you sent to D-hall. He's 17, and was assigned to cut the grass when we go back to our dorm. "Water it to make it grow," he mutters, "and then cut it when it does. That's dumb."

A siren screams far down the two-lane. We watch the sheriff's car speeding toward us. It brakes about thirty feet away, and stops on our side of the road. The flashing light twirls. The sheriff and his deputy stay inside, hidden behind the sun glare on the windshield. A silent EMS ambulance pulls in behind sheriff's car. Uniformed men get out and meet at a spot in the roadside weeds.

Everyone except the Almost Outs rushes to the chain link, and latch fingers into the mesh like they're at the circus or something. Besides Collins, who's picking up picnic trash—and me, because I'm downing the last bottle of spring water—Jerry is the last to saunter over, just bored with sitting still.

An unmarked car comes from the same direction, but slower, and pulls off the road to park behind the ambulance. The sheriff and his deputy cross the ditch, walk a few yards out into a field, and kneel. I join my friends at the fence and we watch the men tug at a round wooden lid and toss it aside. I know it's the cover of an old well. When I came here seven years ago, Collins brought me out here and told me that's where I'd end up if I wasn't a good boy

"Oh-my-god," Steve breathes, his sweaty shoulder bumping mine. "Old Collie's done put some kid in there and he's been found out."

"He told you that, too?" Steve's fourteen, almost two years older than me, and ought to be kidding, trying to scare the Littles. I know from his tense look that he believed the dorm master then, and still does. And they call me Mouse.

Low excited chatter from the guys at the fence. Collins stops picking up ends of hot dog buns and comes over, just in time to see the sheriff take a grappling hook out of his trunk. He hands it to the deputy, who sends it down the well. Collins shoos the smaller boys away from the fence. Now the Almost Outs are coming to see what's so fascinating. Collie puts the Littles into their care and orders them back toward the ivy-covered buildings.

Us Middles watch the deputy bring up a body.

They're too far away for us to see much, but the unmarked car must belong to a private detective or a reporter. He's got a tiny camera and shoots a bunch of pictures before the sheriff marches toward him, waving one arm like an angry drill sergeant.

Reporter or whoever backpedals and sits in his car, watching.

Collins yells at us to get the hell back to our rooms. By ones and twos, the others obey. I linger for a few moments, wondering

6

who she was.   Her skin is a streaky blue, but she's not been down there long enough to rot. One foot still wears a red high heel.

EMS workers put her on a stretcher and load her into the ambulance. It leaves, slowly, and the police car follows. The reporter stares at me. I stare back. Then Collins' shout, too close, burns my ears. "Vincent, get your ass in gear."

I turn, thinking, That's four demerits. D-hall for you, Collie. And I walk away from the fence.

At supper no one's hungry, but we eat it anyway, mostly to keep Collins off our case but partly to cover the chatter over what we'd seen.   What the older and younger inmates think doesn't reach our table, but there's enough nervous joking around me to paint a picture. Collie keeps a tight fist on the television and computer access, so most of what we know from the outside comes in with newbies or Jerry hacking into the Internet in the library. It's the only use he has for my hangout, which is almost always deserted.

"She's a floozy," Jerry says. "Or, was. Who else would end up naked and dead in an abandoned well?"

"Lots of people," Eric says, too mild to provoke Jerry's legendary temper. "I've seen enough tv shows about killers and runaways and wife murderers to be an expert. Anybody can be a victim, not just floozies."

A few other guys add their opinions, some with Jerry, some with Eric. I keep my mouth working on the overcooked green beans and greasy dinner roll.

The dining room is hot even with the windows open. According to Collie, his boss won't let him turn on the air conditioning until summer officially starts—nearly two weeks from now. If it sounds like life here is all bad, it isn't. The buildings are big and old with Masterpiece Theatre woodwork, especially the library. Many of the books are boring, and the encyclopedias are out of date, but there's a pipe-tobacco smell lingering from when some old dude lived in that part of the campus, which was once his house.

There's a swimming pool too, with the Almost Outs assigned lifeguard duty so the rest of us won't drown each other. It opened two days ago, but my swim trunks are too tight so I'll have to borrow Steve's or wait until a busload of us gets a Day Pass to town. Jerry usually misses out on that, being in D-hall much of his life. He's lucky to get a turn at the lame games in the lame game room. At least those don't cost anything to play.

The Visitors' Lobby is the least-used of any area here. Only the Littles get trotted out for potential adopters. It's next to our own student lounge but Collie shuts the French doors connecting the rooms, whenever anybody is over there being interviewed. I remember sitting on a hard chair a few times, trying not to bite my nails or throw up, while young couples who dressed like they had good jobs and presentable relatives would look at me and then at each other. After about age 9, people quit picking my photo out of the Line Up. I guess they want the youngest kid they can find. There's nothing wrong with me, except being shy. And maybe too prone to daydreaming.

My dreaming is interrupted by everyone pushing back chairs and taking their plates to the conveyor belt. Another meal is over, and there's no homework. I look forward to finishing my latest library book, something that must have been smuggled in by an older inmate and has escaped notice. It's a long involved tale about a boy in a European country, who finds a rare book, falls in love with the wrong girl, and has a mysterious stranger following him.

But it doesn't work out that way. When I get back to the room I share with Steve, he's cross-legged on his bunk, noodling on his clarinet. That wouldn't bother me, but Jerry's there, too, draped over my desk chair, and with a look in his eye that never bodes well.

"Shut the door. And be quiet."

I shut the door. Jerry's listening to a little transistor radio, the earpiece keeping his secret until he unplugs it and we hear the newscaster say, ". . . no leads as to the identity of the woman whose body was found Tuesday afternoon in an abandoned well near Hackett. Sheriff A.D. Goodwin says the FBI has been called in to investigate. Turning to the baseball scores —"

"Shit." Jerry clicks off the radio and tosses it aside.

"What did you expect?" Steve asks, dripping spit from the clarinet onto the bare wooden floor. "It's not like she'd be anybody you know."

"With Feds roaming all over the place, I can't put my plan into action."

"What plan is that?" Asking is against my better judgment, but I figure I can spare a few minutes to listen. Jerry has his faults, but boring isn't one of them.

"Get out of this place. A little vacation."

"We're on vacation," I point out.

"If you call mowing and mopping, chopping and dicing, washing and flushing—a vacation."

Since there are no housekeepers, and only one old geezer who doubles as a watchman and groundskeeper, inmates do everything short of a major construction job. "You left out painting," I say, remembering how satisfying it felt to roller on a fresh clean layer.

Steve puts his clarinet back into its case. "Why don't you tell Vinnie about your plan? Maybe he'd be game for it, if you're not."

"The only thing I'm game for is finding out how this story ends." I take the library book from beneath my pillow and adjust myself against the headboard. Before I can hit the lamp switch, Jerry snatches the book from me and peers at the title. Flips through the pages.

"This looks too old for you, Vinn." He places the book under his thigh and lights up a forbidden cigarette.

Steve yells, "Don't do that! Collie will smell it."

"Collie's nose atrophied long ago. He can't smell —"

Steve leaps off his bed and opens the door.

Jerry snubs out the cigarette. Looks at me. "Vinnie, don't you ever want to do something that's fun?"

9

"If you want to leave, leave." I don't mention the likely consequences of going AWOL. Even Jerry hasn't tried that, at least not publicly.

"Steve's onto something here. You, my lad, are so far under the radar that you won't be missed for weeks. You can be our front man, find a place for us to live, maybe line up a couple of jobs. We'll make our break after the case goes cold and the Feds leave town."

Steve cocks his head to one side, the way he does when he's suspicious. "You're not expecting me to do this, are you?"

"We wouldn't have to put up with Collie's ugly mug and storm trooper attitude. Not to mention all the work and lousy food."

Steve gives this some thought. He turns to me. "You are O'Leary's pet. He wouldn't punish you the way he would us, if you were caught."

"I'm not getting caught because I'm not dumb enough to try it. I'm — " I catch myself before blurting out, I'm happy here. For a moment I'm no longer sure this is true. O'Leary is Collins' boss and I'm not his pet. The few times our paths cross is when he's giving out the yearly achievement medals. Mine's always in English and O'Leary dishes up some compliments, that's all. Until tonight I was just going with the flow, but after seeing that dead woman I'm thinking there's a big world out there and I'm missing it. So I finish, " — going to take a shower."

When I get back, Jerry's so into his escape plan that he forgets to tease me about my striped pajamas. What he doesn't know is that I take them off as soon as the light's out. Steve might know, but he'll never tell.

"I'll give you bus fare to the big city of your choice, Mouse. And throw in some cash for eats along the way. And pay for the phone call to tell us where you are. We'll be there ASAP. Won't we, Steve?"

"If you say so."

Steve yawns, but I know he's as wide awake as I am. I decide to play along. "Where would I go? I like a warm climate."

Jerry hunches forward, eager, cheering me on. "Now you're talking. You can do odd jobs, and mail a little traveling money back for us. Since I'm giving you mine."

"Whoa. The first time a letter comes to either of your boxes, Collins traces it back to me."

"He won't know it's money, or from you if you don't do something stupid. Like putting on a return address."

"If I turn up gone, it would be pretty clear. Besides, who else would send you mail? You haven't gotten anything in that box but junk from a porno publisher for two years."

Into the heavy silence that falls, I add, "Of course, I never get any mail at all."

Tight-throat answer as Jerry pushes past me toward the door. "You sure as hell don't. Coward. Baby. Rot in here another six years."

Over the next day or two, we sneak peeks at the news when Collins watches tv in the teachers' lounge. Doesn't look like the Feds will be leaving as soon as I'd hoped, and Jerry is onto me again about tasting adventure. The idea has caught root and is keeping me awake at night.

So on the fourth night after the picnic, with the Feds sending for reinforcements in the case, I find myself wearing a backpack and tennis shoes, a ball cap, and a jacket that's too hot for the night even after a thunderstorm passes.

East Wind is out in the sticks, so the only street lights are the ones on campus, and the only road in either direction is that two lane blacktop that leads into town in one direction and God knows where in the other. Shadows under the ancient oaks move in the slight wind, sending raindrops down on my head, and Jerry casts a ghoulish shadow on the grass as he tries to lasso one of the iron gate points with a nylon rope.

I'm wondering why he chose to send me out by the front instead of down at the chain link, which I think I could climb even if it is higher than this old brick fortress guarding the front. But I shiver, remembering I'd have to pass that well on the road to Hackett, and I can't remember whether the sheriff or his deputy put the cover back on, or not. Chances are I could fall into it in the moonless night. Maybe Jerry thought about that, too, and planned my escape with more concern than I'd given him credit for.

Steve interrupts my musing. "See that little tree? Maybe you could climb it, and go over the wall instead of the gate."

"What if they've got broken glass on top? I read — "

"Quit complaining and get away from here before old Martin comes along." Jerry coils the rope and hands it to me. "Tie the rope to a limb so you can let yourself down."

I climb the tree, tie the rope to a limb, and let myself down onto the uncut grass on the far side of the wall. Behind me, I hear Jerry say, "Get the rope. Don't want to leave any evidence." And Steve answers, "Get it yourself."

While I'm revving up the nerve to leave, Steve runs to the gate. "Hey, Vinnie, you got the money?" He grasps the bars, leans on them.

I walk over to him. Pat my belly. "Pinned to me skivvies."

Jerry joins him, coiling the rope again. "That's your stake, man, and you better not lose it."

"I won't lose it!"

Steve goes through his checklist. "You got the phone number?"

"Pay phone in the dorm—right."

"Remember: hitch to the bus station, and call us the minute you get to the city."

Jerry pulls on his arm. "He knows all that. Come on, let's get inside before somebody closes the damn door."

Steve calls back, "Don't get in the car with anybody you can't beat up."

"Right," I answer, not loud because old Martin might be making his rounds early.

I watch my friends run up the walkway and into the mossy brick building where I've spent more than half my life. The sliver of light winks out as they close the door. Then I jog down the paved road, toward Hackett and away from East Wind.

I've covered half the five miles, grateful that track is one of my electives and I'm in pretty good shape, when I hear Eric's voice saying, "tv shows about killers . . . runaways . . . wife murderers."

The chill inside deepens so even though I'm sweating, I keep the jacket on. Greater than the fear of becoming a victim on tv is the fear of going back to face Jerry. Coward. Crybaby. Mouse.

Nah. It's my first adventure. And the Feds are out there, keeping a lid on things.

Leaving in the middle of the night wasn't such a hot idea. Hackett has one motel, and it's full. A note on the closed key return window says so. Now what?

Episode 2

Snuffling. The backpack jiggles under my head and wakes me. I jerk up, slam against the locked door behind me. My neck is stiff and a damp night on the concrete stoop has lamed one leg. I remember it's a pharmacy, and I see that the snuffler is a German shepherd.

Hey, boy," I say, hoping there isn't a policeman attached anywhere. "You hungry? After my sandwich?"

There is Seeing Eye harness attached to him, but a quick look around doesn't turn up the owner. It's barely past dawn, Sunday morning in Hackett and too early for church. Or anything else.

Didn't sleep much. The plan had been to hitchhike at least part of the way but that hadn't happened. Not a single wild teen in his dad's car, no salesman pulling a red-eye into Hackett. And for sure the little old ladies that I would have accepted a ride from were home snug in bed at 2 a.m. The road was dark and peaceful until it ended at my locked motel, full of out-of-towners covering the investigation.

I unbuckle the pack and unzip the sandwich bag Steve made me take. "You'll be hungry, so here's a midnight snack." Speak for yourself, pal, I never eat after dark in the summer.

Mozart (the first German name that popped into my head, courtesy of Steve and his music idol) wolfs down his part of the peanut butter sandwich. I feel sorry for all the allergic people who don't dare enjoy it. I eat my share while working the tingles out of my foot and the kink out of my neck.

I have a vague idea where the bus station is. I wonder if the dog will follow me. Maybe on the way there'll be a "Lost Dog" poster offering a reward. At least I haven't spent any money on breakfast.

We start in the most likely direction. I'm checking the utility poles for something besides old yard sale signs when I hear a faint whistle and a worried voice calling, "Macho! Macho! Here, boy, where are you? Come back, Macho."

A male voice, probably not searching for a lost kid with a name like that. I stop and the dog stops with me. "You going to answer him, or aren't you, Macho?"

The voice is coming from the next alley. Macho-Mozart just looks up at me, pink tongue lolling out, hope in his eyes. "Want another sandwich? Sorry but I'm fresh out."

"Is someone there?" A man about thirty, dressed in slacks and a polo shirt, feels his way into view with a cane. He's wearing dark glasses, and old Mouse puts two and two together.

"I'm here," I answer. "And I have Macho. I think."

"Thank God!" He hunkers and holds out a hand. Macho goes to him. He hooks an old-fashioned leather leash on the harness and stands up. "Thank you —?"

His voice asks for a name and I almost say it but catch myself. "No problem." I start to walk away but the man keeps talking.

"I got a little turned around, I'm afraid. Can you take me to the bus station?"

Even with the dog he looks helpless, and since I'm going there and he won't know if I make a few wrong turns, I say, "Sure."

We walk along the deserted streets. I watch for a bus station sign, and he talks my ear off. "Macho's young and still in training. The last dog I had would never run away and leave me, but he grew old and went into retirement. I miss him, but Macho learns quickly and will grow old with me."

The man's name is Al, and he's meeting a friend at the Morningbird Hotel in Fairview

I look for buses on the street or parked in a lot. Al says, "I've been to the hotel, but it's been awhile. Do you suppose you could go there with me? I'll be happy to pay your fare."

A few things go through my head, but what comes out of my mouth is, "I have a fifteen minute stop over in Fairview." Steve's bus schedule has little red circles along a thin red line, all the way to Dentonville, where we're to meet next week.

"What serendipity! A fellow traveler. How much farther to the station?"

At that moment I spot a bus rounding a corner up ahead, and follow it. "Not far," I say, hoping it's the truth.

Two more blocks and we're entering a convenience store with a hand-lettered sign "bus" in the window. I smell coffee and my mouth starts to water, but what I really want is cold orange juice. My friend taps his way to the counter as if he's done this before, and makes good on his promise to pay the part of my fare that takes me to his destination. I thank him, even if I am returning the favor.

"Bus for Fairview leaves in thirty minutes," the clerk reminds us. Al says, "If you want refreshments, machines are around the corner." Macho guides him to an empty table near the rest rooms. "Bring me a coffee, will you? Black."

The machines in the corridor dispense coffee, juice, and candy. I take a tray and load it with drinks and five candy bars. It's brunch time at East Wind and right now my pals are feasting on omelets and pancakes and reading the comics. When I get to Fairview, I'm going to find a diner, so I stuff the candy into my pockets and return to our table. Macho lies at his master's feet,

15

rolling his eyes at me in that way dogs have. "Chocolate isn't good for canines," I tell him.

Al's left handed. I watch him place and find his Styrofoam cup between gulps. I notice that he's unhooked the leash and put it in his pocket. I want to ask if he's been blind all his life, but it seems a nosy question.

A bus pulls in, hissing to a stop out front. The driver changes his sign from Hackett to Fairview. "That's ours. Do you need any help?"

"Just guide me by the elbow." Al fumbles and finds Macho's harness handle, and we go outside with several other people who are leaving town. Nobody has gotten off, and only a handful remain seated for points farther along the route.

I let go of Al's elbow so he can reach for the grab bar. On his other side, Macho leaps away as if he's seen a squirrel or a cat and races down the sidewalk. I leap after him but someone grabs the backpack, jerking me to a stop. It's Al, and I'm confused. I try to see where Macho went, and then I try to see through the man's dark glasses. It's hard to know what a person is thinking when you can't see his eyes.

"The driver'll wait until I can bring him back."

"No, I don't want to cause trouble. Get on. Macho will go home and my neighbor will see that he's taken care of."

"But what will you do— "

Al shows our tickets and steers me ahead of him into a seat near the middle. "I'll be fine, once I'm in the lobby of the Morningbird."

The bus is noisy and the driver seems to be making up for lost time. We speed around curves that throw Al and me together, first one way and then the other. He stares straight ahead, but the sunglasses are curved and his eyes are hidden. I've never known a blind person before, would the lids be open or closed?

His lips smile, as if his thoughts are pleasant. Mine are divided. I worry about Macho, then I worry that maybe Al's friend won't show up and I'll be stuck doing my good deed for

16

another hour before he can get a return bus. I promise myself I'll stick to the plan and leave the Boy Scouting to the next twirp.

At least I'm clear of Hackett and the dead woman and anybody at East Wind that might realize I'm gone. I lean my head on the seat and doze.

The buzzer sounds, jarring me out of a dream about pancakes. I'm five and it's my last Christmas with my family. Even then I knew nobody was happy, but I didn't know why. I still don't.

The bus brakes in front of an old brick building that looks like an apartment complex that got left behind. Weeds grow in cracks in the parking lot, and dirty white paint curls in strips from the wood trim around windows and doors. There are posts but the sign no longer hangs between them.

I'm waiting to see who's getting off here, when Al's fingers clamp on my arm and he leads me into the aisle. I'm saying, "This can't be right! Driver, we're going to the Morningbird Hotel."

"This is it, son." The bus driver revs the engine, a signal to hurry up. Nobody else moves or answers, and Al forces me down the bus steps.

The bus pulls away while I'm trying to make sense of this.

"We should have stayed on. It must be miles into town."

"I know what I'm doing." Al jerks me along the walkway and up a few steps into the building. "Just stay calm. I'm not going to hurt you."

The peanut butter sandwich churns halfway up before it settles into an uneasy knot in my stomach. The lobby is worse than the outside. Dirt and trash everywhere. I twist my arm to free it, but his grip bruises the flesh all the way to the bone. "You are hurting me."

He pulls a cell phone from his pocket and speed dials somebody. Now I'm thinking, Damn, old Collie sicced the Feds on me before I can even have breakfast in that diner. I wonder how I could have been so stupid. Steve warned me against making any friends or being noticed by anybody who could give my description to a cop or reporter. I should have run from Al as soon as he came out of that alley. And I know I have to get away from him or go back and be laughed at for the rest of my life, at least the part of it I'll have to spend at East Wind.

He lets go of my arm, certain that I can't get help in this godforsaken place. I try to remember if the bus made any major turns between Hackett and here. It must be halfway to noon now. I figure here is closer to Fairview so I'll have to keep going in the same direction and hope I don't get lost. Then I start paying attention to what he's saying.

He paces, the phone to his left ear. "I told you I'd get him and I did. Where the hell are you? I can't hang around all day. Half an hour, buddy, if you want him. You'd better have the money."

Half an hour. I can jog that long without being winded. Thankful that it's not Al I need to worry about, I dash for the door he's left open. He's quick and his tackle knocks me to the floor. He's picking me up by the backpack and I'm yelling, "Stop bruising the merchandise!"

The dark glasses sit crooked on his face, one earpiece bent. His free hand flips them off. He grins at me. His eyes are wide open, a fanatic pale blue. But not blind. Suddenly I realize what this deal is. He's brought me to a dark and ugly place for a dark and ugly deed. He laughs. Then he drags me up some stairs and puts me in the bedroom of a 2-room suite. Locks the door between us. The click activates the urge to throw up again but I concentrate on his muffled conversation, he's losing patience.

"Yeah he's just your type. You'd better hurry. My time will cost you extra."

At least it's not him, but someone else. Someone else, coming in a hurry. There used to be a slide latch on this side, the screw holes and different paint outline are all that's left so I can't lock myself in. Who would rescue me, if I did? Besides, two determined guys would just break down the door. I look around for possibilities.

One window, old fashioned and breakable, but aside from a dresser that was ancient when O'Leary was a kid, there's nothing to break it with other than my backpack.   I cross to it. Part of a wooden fire escape clings to the building. There's a small weedy field with a line of trees beyond. Safe under that dense cover in less than five minutes. If I can get the window open.

Painted a few times, so tugging is useless. It's gone quiet in the other room and my heart thuds and skips, my nerves shot. Sweat stings my eyes as I run the blade of my pocket knife around the edges, breaking loose the sickly yellow gunk. At last I push the frame up enough to crawl through, thankful there's no wire screen to deal with, and praying it doesn't fall on me and break a rib or worse.

The fire escape landing outside has rotted away. Jumping to the ground is risky and might send me to the hospital with a broken foot.

I toss down the bulky backpack. It thumps and bounces out of sight. Thankful the builders of the Morningbird Hotel didn't add a third story, I take off my leather belt with the steer head buckle that I won in the spring essay contest. Straddle the window ledge. Lean out and loop the belt on the lowest bit of railing I can reach. At least this way my hands won't get infected from the splintery timbers.

In the room behind me I hear the door open. "Hey! What the hell do you think you're doing?" Running footsteps.

I lean out and take hold of the belt and am one-leg-over the window ledge when Al grabs my ankle.

"Get back in here! You trying to kill yourself?"

He's got me by my jeans leg. Hanging mostly upside down, I don't dare let go of the belt because then he'll pull me back inside. We struggle for a while and then rest. Time ticks away like the sweat dripping from my hair into my eyes. "Stand off," I taunt. "Let me go and I won't report you."

He laughs again and gives a jerk that nearly tears me in two. I twist the other leg up over the ledge and kick at his hands, unable to reach his face. The sneaker on my captured foot feels like it's going to slip over my heel. My jeans feel like they're slipping too. Bracing my free foot against the building gives me leverage to slide Al forward under the window sash. Wishing the thing would fall on him doesn't work.

Then the cell phone rings in his shirt pocket, startling him just enough that his grip fails and I break loose. Leaving my belt behind, I drop through the broken landing and sooner than I'm ready my feet hit the ground below. I snatch up my backpack and try to think which way to flee. He'll see me in the field, or on the road, but going back inside I'd be trapped. Especially if the man coming to claim me arrives before I'm clear of this place.

Al has left the window. He has to be coming down the stairs, and the direct route to me is down a main hallway and out the door opening on the pool area.

I take a chance and try the door right beside me under the fire escape. It leads down a short dark hallway to what was once a kitchen. The kitchen is next to a dining area, and the dining area ought to be near the lobby. I give Al time to clear the main hallway to the back, then I duck through the lobby, out the front door, and into thick woods across the road.

I fight through underbrush, through little trees close together, then bigger trees with high canopies, then little ones again. Pausing in the underbrush on the far side of the woods, my throat and lungs burn and my knees wobble. My sneaker has worked its way back into place, and I still have my pack. I sit down on it to catch my breath. The candy inside has probably melted all over my clothes. At this point, I'm not hungry and don't want to find out if that's the case.

There's another field, beyond a two-lane leading somewhere. Will it take me back to the Morningbird, or will the first car I see coming toward me be Al's client? I have to keep traveling. Which way?

Then I spot a pickup truck moving along another road at the far edge of the field. I shoulder my backpack and am on the run again.

Episode 3

By the time I reach the other road, the pickup truck's almost out of sight. Nothing in the other direction, so I trot after it. Half an hour later there it sits in the gravel parking lot of a cafe with a neon "open" sign and steam or smoke coming out of a chimney. Suddenly I'm starving.

It's been at least 15 hours since I had any real food, and after what I've been through, I'd fight a trucker for a piece of fried chicken or anything Italian. Or a breakfast with three eggs, bacon, and lots of coffee even though I don't usually get to drink it at East Wind.

Typical roadside cafe, with stools at a counter and a few square tables scattered between it and the windows. One middle-aged lady cook scraping down the grill, her single customer smoking on the last stool near the door. I plant myself at the other end and look at the poorly-typed menu. Little bits of paper with new prices are stuck over the old.

I study the inked-in numbers, aware that the $185 that Jerry gave me for a stake is a limited resource. "You can get a weekly special at this Dentonville motel for $125," he'd said, giving me a printout from the Internet, "and do odd jobs until you parlay the rest into a couple hundred."

I was only now beginning to see the fallacy in the plan. If I work for a week and make back $125, that would pay only for a place to sleep. Adding in meals, I'll be left without enough to call home, let alone send cash to the two friends who've gotten me into this. What was I thinking?

Math has never been my strong point, but I'm fast learning about people. At East Wind there are all types, but nobody is dangerous, unless you count Jerry who does have a mean streak. He's probably laughing his ass off right now, waiting for me to come slinking back and in his debt for whatever money I've spent.

"What'll you have, son?" the cook asks.

"Coffee. And a plain burger. Burn it." It's the cheapest thing on the menu, and those chocolate bars, squashed and melted or not, are likely to be supper.

The clock on the wall startles me. Hands point to three-fifteen. "Is that clock right?" She glances at it and nods. I'm floored. Except for my late-night snooze on the pharmacy stoop, and a nap on the bus, I've been up for over thirteen hours, most of it running for my life, or at least my freedom. The coffee barely steadies my hand.

But I got away from Al, and I can do this. Jerry underestimated my ingenuity. My order arrives and I'm happily guzzling coffee when the driver of the pickup truck pays his bill and leaves with a wave to the lady behind the counter. She says, "See ya Clarence," and then she stares into some long thoughts or memories. My eyes check the driver's dessert dish but nothing's left, not even crumbs.

As he passes through the door, another man comes in. This one is short and stocky, about thirty. He sits on the same stool. His dark hair is cut short behind but long on top, slicked straight back without a part. He's wearing slacks and a black t-shirt with no logo. He looks like an actor.

I eat the plain burger slowly, making the most of each bite, remembering the picnic. Wishing myself back there, with it all to do over again. I'd probably help old Collie pick up the trash, give him a thrill. Smiling, I take the refill she offers.

She turns on a little tv hanging on the wall behind the cash register. No sound, just the video. After a minute a special news bulletin flashes and my heart starts pounding. But instead of a posse fanning out to search for a nobody runaway from the boys' school, it's the reporter's stills of the sheriff's deputy draped in a dead blonde body. He was closer to the scene of the action than we were, so her single red shoe hits me harder now than when I saw it for real.

Worse, there's a shot of her face. Her half-shut eyes seem to be looking around at the camera.

The actor makes a choking sound, loud enough that the cafe lady looks around, wide-eyed-fearful that she'll have a dead customer on her hands because she never learned the Heimlich maneuver. His attention is fixed on the tv and he's motionless, not threshing around in agony, but his voice is gravelly when he says, "Turn that up."

She does. The reporter is in the news room. "If you know this woman, please call—" He gives the number, which appears over and over at the bottom of the screen, like a weather warning, and then regular programming resumes. Actor keeps watching with a dazed look on his face, replaying what he's seen, unable to believe it. I almost tell him, "I was there," but a new caution keeps my mouth closed. He knows her, I'd bet half my stake on it.

I wait for him to go to the pay phone outside, but he finally breaks his trance and pushes food around on his plate. He has a refill.

When the cafe lady raises the nearly empty pot toward me, I shake my head. Too much coffee will make me need to pee an hour from now, when I'm on the way to Dentonville. It's a farm road, like the rest that Jerry said would be safer to travel than an interstate. Finishing my meal, I'm more relaxed than I've been since Jerry routed me out of bed, with a theatrical whisper, "It's time, Mouse."

She puts the bill face down beside my plate. Telling Steve the money was "pinned to me skivvies" was a joke. I feel in my jeans pocket for the folded greenbacks. A chill engulfs me. I hear Jerry warn, "Don't lose it!" and I hear my defensive answer, "I won't lose it!" I feel in the other pocket, then open the backpack to check the jacket, even though I'm sure I never moved it. But it isn't there, or in the jacket, or loose in the pack.

It's on that broken landing. Jiggled out of my pocket when Al was dangling me upside down. If it had fallen through the broken landing, I'd've seen it on the ground below. Al wouldn't have noticed it beneath the window, he was set on getting downstairs and heading me off.

23

I swallow against a dry throat. Take a drink of the lemon-flavored water. The Morningbird is miles behind me. The bill for lunch stares up at me. If I had the energy to flee, I would.

Stalling, I pretend to drink more water. Try to think but my brain has turned to cotton candy, all fluff and too much sugar. Bad enough to run out on a poor woman who probably sunk her money into this place and is barely scraping by. Worse to realize that my cushion of comfort is lying in the ruins of a place I'd rather never see again. And worst of all, if I don't get that money back I can't even return to East Wind with my tail between my legs.

The harder I try not to cry, the harder it is to control my breathing, never mind the tears leaking out of my eyes. Not daring to blow my runny nose and draw attention, I wipe it on a sandpaper napkin. Then the devious part of my brain kicks in. I dig a pen from my pack and write I will be back! on the bill. Then I add, with money.

Hoping that will be the case, I drop off the stool and head for the rest room. In a rinkydink place like this, there ought to be a window that opens, one I can climb through.

There is, and I do. It's high, but there's a metal trash can that I can stand on, and I don't need to use my knife to loosen old paint because there's only one layer. Hanging onto window ledges is getting to be a habit, but this one is ground level and I take off like a jet through the weedy lot between here and the woods. Retracing my flight pattern isn't hard. The broken brush and trail of footsteps in soft ground lead me to the Morningbird in little more than half the time it took to follow the pickup truck to the cafe.

Lurking in the fringe of underbrush, I feel like a juvenile detective from one of the series books in our library, casing the joint. No cars parked out front, nothing moving except the tree branches bending in a rising wind. Long minutes pass. Dark clouds move overhead. Finally I figure Al and his man have either left or killed each other, but what are the odds of my finding another dead body in the same week?

Dumping the pack so I can run fast, I dart across the two-lane and hunker behind an overgrown bush. Through its swaying branches I can see the parking lot, which is empty. There's no other cover to shield my movements. I take a few deep breaths, shake my arms and legs to limber them for the effort, and race to the back of the building.

That was dumb. The fire escape landing is too high to reach, too flimsy to climb. My belt still hangs where I left it a few hours earlier. Hoping I was wrong about where the folded bills might have fallen, I search beneath the structure. Not here.

I enter the dark hallway that leads to the kitchen. Eerily quiet. No angry voices, no groaning, no footsteps. I creep along, tense as a prey animal, half expecting Al to leap out and gnash me with vampire teeth. But I reach the stairs and ease myself upward from tread to tread, holding my breath after each creak and squeak. Along the dim hallway I find the door to the room Al locked me in, and on shaky knees tiptoe to the open window.

I look out, ready to scoop up my money and run.

It isn't there, either.

I step through the window and search the cracks in the boards that remain attached to the framework. Once, forgetting the hole behind me, I nearly fall through but catch the belt and save myself from a nasty injury. More careful, I unbuckle the belt and while I'm feeling it through the belt loops I wonder if I can sell or pawn it.

I wonder if Al did see the money and came back after it. I wonder how much his customer had been willing to pay him for a toy boy. I thank Jerry for adding that term to my education. I wonder if he knew it because something like this had happened to him before he was put in East Wind. Would I be better off if the cafe lady were my mother and I lived with her, just us two against the world, and went to a public school and watched tv whenever I wanted, and checked out public library books? And had friends that didn't think it was funny to make a fool of me.

After one last look around, with no better results, I'm halfway downstairs when the storm hits. Safer inside than out, I find a second-floor room that still has a bed and mattress, and with lightning playing through the windows, I'm asleep in moments.

I wake to pitch dark. The rain and wind have stopped. At first I think I've dreamed everything, but that doesn't wash because if I was in my bed, there'd be light under the door and Steve snoring in the opposite corner of our room. His honks and snorks didn't wake me, so what did? I'm frozen by an unnamed fear. Listening for whatever went bump in the night, or cars passing in the road, I hear a distant wailing that starts in the yard and comes toward the Morningbird.

Downstairs a door slams and I shoot upright, my heart thumping so hard it hurts. Running footsteps vanish in the lobby, yet the wailing echoes up the stairwell. My first thought is to scoot under the bed, but since there's a metal fire escape on this end of the motel, out the window I go. Clouds still cover the moon. Or maybe it's already set, I've lost all sense of time.

In the back parking lot, there's the bulk of a car that wasn't here before. I can't make out what kind it is, but the shape screams old. My sleeping mind must have heard it arrive and kicked me into consciousness. Through the open window that terrible wailing continues, from deep in the darkness of the motel. I don't believe in ghosts, especially the kind that drive a car, but the sound cuts through me and I streak over the weedy yard and across the deserted road. Running ahead of the track team toward the finish line, the cheap trophy cup almost in my hand.

Not knowing where else to go, I head back through the rain-drenched woods toward the cafe. Staying at the Morningbird one more moment would be the stupidest thing I've done so far.

She's closed the rest room window, and there's no metal trash can outside to boost me up. There is a small utility building, with a lock on the door. Walking around the cafe, I peer through the glass and see the lighted clock. Two a.m. again. I've come full circle, with nothing to show for it except aches and bruises and an empty stomach.

Tossing the pack down in the shelter of the doorway, I start to sit on it but before I do that I take out one of the squashed candy bars. It's filled with coconut, my favorite. Leaves me thirsty. A bright beacon of a drink machine beckons, but lacking even coins for that, I settle down to wait for the nice lady to come open her cafe

"Good Lord, you again!"

Struggling to a sitting position, I blink into a misty dawn. The tired, stern person standing before me causes a surge of guilt. "Yes, Ma'am. I'm sorry, I meant to pay you, but I lost my money."

"Well you don't look like a drinker or gambler. Were you robbed?"

She unlocks the door and I follow her inside. "In a manner of speaking," I answer. She goes behind the counter and lights her stove burners. Puts on an apron. Washes her hands at a sink. Takes stuff out of a freezer and finds room for it in a cooler. It's pretty certain she's going to offer me breakfast instead of calling the police. I perch on the stool I occupied yesterday and wait to see what develops.

"Wasn't it awful about that woman over in Hackett," she remarks, getting the coffee started. She mixes up what I hope is pancake batter.

"Awful," I agree. "I'd hate to fall in a well."

"Oh, that poor soul never fell in. She was murdered. I don't doubt, some man took out his rage on her. No rich-looking person like her would be walking in the weeds in hundred-dollar shoes."

I remember that the sheriff lifted an old cover from the well. Somebody had been careful to replace it. I wonder who tipped the cops off so they knew where she was, or if looking in old wells is just a part of searching for a missing person. I wonder why the Feds were called in so soon.

"Young to be out all by yourself," the cafe owner says. "Never seen you around before."

27

"I'm on my way to Dentonville. Hiking," I add. "For my Scout badge." That explanation comes out so easily I'm amazed, but figure it's as good as anything to reinforce my image.

"You got a long way to go. Fifty miles at least."

"Does a bus stop here?" She gives me a short stack and three squares of real butter. I reach for the plastic jar of honey. I need to get far away, where the news of Hackett can't reach me. Or the police, who must be on my trail by now.

"Used to. The Interstate killed everything on this road and the next over. Just locals now. You might hitch a ride with Clarence as far as Parker City."

Parker City wasn't one of Steve's red circles. I'd remember if it was. I take out the map, wipe off a smear of chocolate, and am shocked to see that I must have slept longer than I realized during the bus ride with Al. I've landed 50 miles beyond Dentonville.

But this is only the second day, and I'm getting the hang of taking care of myself. She keeps my coffee cup brimming and hot. The meal revives me, clears my thinking. "I'll be happy to wash everything in here for a bit of cash."

"How much?" Her voice takes on a suspicious edge.

"To pay for the food, and maybe a burger to go." Asking for more seems cruel, considering her circumstances. Besides, hitching with Clarence will save me bus fare.

Two hours later, everything is sparkling clean when a couple of regulars take seats at a table and order the breakfast specials. Clarence hasn't shown up. She calls his house but he doesn't answer. "He might have gone to Fletcher," she says. "With a load of produce."

She clicks on the tv again and the news isn't good. People are still being asked to call this number if they know the woman found dead near Hackett. The second clip is worse still, but it doesn't involve me, so I turn in my mop and pail, and the lady gives me ten dollars.

"Don't spend it all in one place," she jokes, with a sad smile. When she hands me a bag containing a can drink and a burger all the way, I try to pay for yesterday's lunch, but she refuses. "I had a kid like you once."

My throat closes on the question. It's none of my business what happened to him, or why.

I leave the cafe behind, heading toward Dentonville. Other thoughts fly around in my head like bats. "Don't get in the car with anybody you can't beat up," Steve had warned me. Good advice. Next time, I won't be so trusting.

Four hours and approximately fifteen miles later, I come to a burg with a few houses, main street, and a large park. My feet are tired, it's hot, and I'm ready for my lunch. Finding a shaded picnic table, I unpack and am chowing down when a sleek SUV pulls in and two passengers cross the grass toward me. The driver is dressed like a wannabe rock star in tattered jeans and sandals, and the girl riding shotgun could be a wannabe singer in a flowing white dress. He looks to be in his twenty's, she's maybe sixteen.

"Hey, dude, I'm Hoodoo." He holds out a hand for me to shake it and I notice that his clothes aren't just recently dirty like mine, but old dirty like he hasn't changed them in days. The girl is clean and she's lazily brushing her long, shiny hair. "I'm Francine," she says, "but you can call me Franny." They sit down on the bench opposite me. She kicks off white leather sandals, puts her feet against Hoodoo's thigh, nudges him playfully.

It's only then that I see a third person emerging from the SUV. He slams the door like he's pissed and walks to us carrying a medium-sized cooler. He's better looking than Hoodoo, his age somewhere between the other two, who giggle and flirt as if nobody else is around. His shirt came from an upscale store, so did the running shoes. His short curly hair is the same brown shade as Franny's. She says, "This old man is Ernie. He's blood kin, can you tell?"

"You do look alike," I say cautiously.

"Haul it out and let's get this over," Hoodoo tells her. "I've never seen people that eat as often as you do."

"Only winos get by on as little as you eat," Ernie shoots back at him.

Hoodoo flips Ernie the bird, and I watch her unpack the cooler. The ice has mostly melted and water drips from the plastic containers as she puts them on the table. Hoodoo opens one and sniffs the contents. Dumps it on the ground. Opens two more. Same fate. He grabs his head in both hands and shouts, "You trying to kill us?"

Francine picks up the containers and throws them into the nearest big rusty trash can.

"Hey!" Hoodoo rescues a beer from the bottom of the cooler. He pops the top and takes a long swig.

Ernie's been sitting beside me, watching the show. "We have anything to drink besides beer?"

"A quart of grape juice. Under my seat in the SooV."

Ernie goes back toward the SUV. "Bring those Styrofoam cups," his sister calls after him. "I want some, too." She washes her hands in the water fountain, dries them on her dress. Turns to me. "We're a new gen," she says. "Hipsies. You know what that means? Hippy gypsies. I made that up."

"I made that up," Hoodoo corrects her. He paces in a tight little circle, downing the beer like it's a contest he intends to win. Turns to me. "You hoofin' it?"

"What?" I'm watching Ernie examine the cups he's brought back.

"You know—running away. On foot. Hoofin' it."

I know better than to trust a guy called Hoodoo with the truth, but this time the hiking Boy Scout lie gets stuck in my throat and I'm left with my mouth hanging open. One thing I've decided, though, is to ride as far as I can with them. So long as it's toward Dentonville.

Episode 4

I try for a balance between eager and pathetic. "I'm meeting friends in Dentonville. Any chance you're headed there?"

Hoodoo laughs. "I'm headed to Hollywood. Going to be in a movie."

"Yeah," Ernie says, "a horror movie."

Franny grabs Hoodoo's arm before he can land a blow. "Come on, babe, help me look for money." Hoodoo slaps his thigh and does a little rain dance. "Now that's a hoot!" They walk off down a path hugged up so tight they can hardly walk.

"Want some juice? One hundred per cent all natural." Ernie offers the quart container. The glass is warm from being under the seat. "Watch those cups. Hoodoo likes to chew his."

I examine the Styrofoam cups he brought from the SUV. "They're all chewed." I pick the one that has a clean side and Ernie fills it. The juice reminds me how hungry I still am, but if I break out those candy bars Hoodoo would probably take them away from me.

"You ought to go home." Ernie stares after his sister. She and Hoodoo have turned a corner and we can't see them for the bushes.

"Can't." I drink from the cup.

"Why not?'

"A matter of honor."

He turns his head, smiling a little. "Really?"

"Are you guys going toward Dentonville?"

"With Hoodoo, you never know. Why, you got a deadline?"

"Yeah. Actually, I have."

He smiles at me again, like he's thinking something pleasant for a change. I decide I like Ernie, but to be on the safe side, I add, "Those friends are expecting me."

Franny and Hoodoo come back, hand in hand. He says, "Take a walk, you two."

Ernie stands up from the picnic table seat. "Fran, don't you think — "

Hoodoo thumbs us away and walks to the SUV. Franny says to us, "Go on. There's a duck pond just around that curve. With ducks." She follows him into the back and shuts the door. I notice there are curtains over every window, and they plaster a sun guard over the windshield.

Ernie's pleasant mood has passed but he's more sad than mad. "Come on, kid, let's walk off some calories."

"Call me Vinnie," I tell him. I may be a kid but I don't like being reminded of it. "Grape juice has calories?"

We follow the path to the curve before he stops and looks back at the SUV. He picks up a golf-ball-sized rock and flings it in a high arc. Of course it falls short, but the effort seems to make him feel better.

"You guys don't get along very well, do you."

"The day we start getting along, I'll kill myself."

We round the curve and can't see the SUV or the picnic table. I realize I left my backpack there and my heart thumps a time or two before it settles into its normal pace.

"Guess we've gone far enough," Ernie says.

"I don't see any pond. Or ducks."

He ruffles my hair the way he would do a little brother. "Don't believe everything Fran says."

We keep walking, though, round another curve and there's the pond. Three brown ducks paddle about, scooping up something, probably insects or floating weeds. I make a mental note to read up on ducks the first chance I get.

"Well, maybe half of what she says," Ernie tells me with a wry grin.

We sit on the grass and watch the ducks. I worry about the backpack. Then I laugh because there's nothing in it but a change of clothes and a few battered chocolate bars. I wonder what happened to Jerry's money.

Ernie stares out over the water to the fringe of houses beyond. "Vinnie, are you a happy person?"

I ponder that. "I was."

"What happened?"

Again I counter his question with one of my own. "Who is Hoodoo?"

"He's the bastard Fran thinks she's in love with." Ernie's voice trembles and he heaves a rock into the pond like he'd gladly use Hoodoo's head for a target.

The words didn't tell me anything I hadn't guessed, but opened up all kinds of lines of inquiry. "You're on a mission, too."

"A matter of honor," he says, and stands up. "We can go back now."

The picnic table and SUV come into view. Hoodoo's sitting on it and Fran's stuffing more things into the trash can. I pick up my backpack, and remember that there is something valuable inside other than my jacket. At the last minute before leaving East Wind, I'd packed my camera. An old one, uses a cartridge, but it takes good pictures.

Hoodoo gets into the driver's seat, Fran beside him. Ernie's in the back, holding the door open. "You with us or not?"

I am.

Dentonville, here I come. What I'll do when I get there, I haven't a clue. Beg, I suppose. Beg for a job, beg for a room, beg for food. Pawn my camera? One thing I can't do is use my real name or break down and cry and sob out the whole sordid story.

Trying to sort out a better lie than the one about being a hiking Boy Scout, I take the camera from the pack and hold it in my lap. I think about the worn photo in my cashless wallet. It's my mother, taken before I was born. I don't know anything about her family, or my dad or his family. Even my memories are featureless now, like the picture. I wonder if I was happy once, with them. Funny. I was happy at East Wind.

While my attention wandered, I missed seeing what road Hoodoo took in leaving the park, and watch unsuccessfully for any road sign that might tell me how far we are from where I'm going, or even where we are. Fields and woods take turns bordering the two-lane, with farm houses scattered along the route, most set in a grove of old trees, with dirt roads leading to them. "Wake me up when we get to Dentonville," I tell Ernie, but he's in his own little world.

Fran says something that almost pulls me out of my stupor, and I hear Hoodoo's answer. "I'm waiting for rich boy to say he'll treat us."

Ernie's voice carries a warning note. "I'm keeping track of all this freeloading." And Hoodoo fires back, "Nobody asked you along, crudball."

Don't know how long I've been asleep, but I'm thrown against Fran's seat as the SUV makes a sharp swerve and a sudden stop. Next time I'll use the seat belt. Shadows are long but the sky is still light. Well, it would be, in June. Summer's here. Steve and Jerry must be trying to outdo each other swimming laps in the pool at East Wind. My stomach thinks it's close to supper time.

Fran's peevish voice finishes dragging me to full consciousness. "I didn't mean for you to give us all whiplash."

"You wanted to stop. I stopped. Quit bitching."

Hoodoo's at the end of some rope. That makes me uneasy. Ernie rouses up as if he's been sleeping too. "What are we supposed to eat in a place like this?"

'Like this' turns out to be a gravel space in front of a long-abandoned service station. Three decades ago, at least. At a crossroads with no signs, and not a thing visible in any direction except fields bordered by woods, or woods close to the road.

Fran opens her door. "I didn't want to eat, I want to pee."

I do, too, but not here. The building is falling apart, unstable enough to collapse on unwary visitors. Watching Fran pick her way to the back, I ask, "What time is it?" Ernie doesn't have to look at his watch to tell me, "After seven o'clock."

Seven o'clock! We've been driving over five hours. Hoodoo distracts me from a confused panic with a weird comment: "I hate Daylight Savings Time."

Ernie says in a tired voice, "You hate everything."

"Mostly you." Hoodoo opens his door, lights a cigarette, waits for Fran to come back.

"That sentiment is mutual, pal."

Opening my door, I think about taking a picture of the place. Ernie continues in the same vein. "Close my eyes for one minute and you screw things up."

"Fran's the navigator, I'm the driver. Can I help it if she reads the damn map upside down?"

Fran's back, and leans into his chest, wrapping her arms around his neck. "Well, according to your map, we were going upside down."

Hoodoo shrugs her off and barks, "See? What kind of a fool statement is that?" He pushes past her and stomps off toward the back of the building. Fran sits in the driver's seat, not looking at either of us. Ernie begins, "Fran, please — " but she interrupts, "Don't start."

She walks away, makes aimless circles around the parking lot. Looking for money, maybe. After a minute Ernie climbs out past me and goes toward her. I climb out too, to stretch my legs and maybe take a pee after all. My camera's hanging by its strap around my neck, and I figure I'll try to get their picture. Make sure all this banging around and being dropped hasn't broken the working parts of it.

Looking through the viewfinder, I step from side to side, then forward, searching for a shot that won't pick up sun glare or plant a tree in the top of their heads. I'm maybe eight feet away when Hoodoo enters the picture. I watch him give Ernie a flat-handed push away from Fran. I see Fran grab Hoodoo's arm.

Ernie's hand shoots out, returning the chest-push. Hoodoo's off balance for a moment. Fran grabs at Ernie's arm. My finger jerks, tensing, and the shutter clicks — just as Hoodoo's fist crashes into Ernie's jaw. He can't dodge because Fran's holding him, but the force of the blow sends him backwards out of her grasp. He sprawls on the ground.

I drop the camera from my eye. Hoodoo grabs Fran's wrist and runs to the SUV, dragging her with him. She stumbles, and

Hoodoo picks her up and tosses her onto her seat and slams the door. Runs around to his open door and leaps in. Fires up the engine, and backs a swift half-circle around Ernie, still spread-eagled on his back. A lurch into forward gear and the SUV tears away, throwing gravel that hits my legs like little hailstones. I note which of the crossroads they take, then run to Ernie.

"Are you hurt?"

He's moving around, groggy but able to sit up. Touches the back of his head. Winces. "Ow! Am I bleeding?" Looks at his fingers. "I am!"

I peer at his head where he's holding a part in the hair. "Yeah, a little bit."

He stands up, shaky. "Gravel took a chunk out." Touches his jaw. "Nearly broke my jaw, too. Bastard."

Now that I know he's mobile, I look around us with fresh eyes and my heart nearly stops. "Where are we?"

Ernie looks around, too. "Damned if I know."

"Weren't you awake?"

"No," he tells me, irritated. "I've been going on no sleep for three days." He feels his head and wipes his fingers on his jeans.

"That's how long you've been traveling with them?"

"Ever since Hoodoo brainwashed my brainless sister into taking Dad's SUV on a 'vacation.'"

"Must be the moon," I mutter. In spite of the coming night, I feel safe with Ernie. I wonder whether Hoodoo was lost most of the time we'd been driving, which would mean we weren't as far from civilization as we would be if he just drove nonstop for almost six hours. "Where were you guys really headed?"

"To hell, apparently." Ernie heaves a long sigh, assessing each of our choices of route out. There are no signs to tell us where we've been or where we might end up. Even the service station sign is so weathered we can't read the once-red letters.

"When it gets dark," I suggest, "we can see house lights a long way off. Or a car will pass and pick us up."

He turns to me, his lean face lit by spears of sun cutting through tree branches. "You little optimist." His smile is fleeting. "Did you see which way they went?"

"Yeah." I start out walking, Ernie beside me. It's then that I realize I don't need to pee any more. I hope he doesn't notice the wet crotch or the smell.

He's occupied with feeling in his pockets. "Damn!

"What?"

"One of them stole my credit card."

"You have a bank account?"

"I did have."

We have nothing but the clothes we're in and my camera slung around my neck. Hoodoo — or Fran, more likely — will discover my chocolate bars and eat them. The thought of melting chocolate on my tongue makes me thirsty. I long for the machine in our dorm at East Wind, which dispenses pint bottles of real spring water.

I consider going back to the service station before we get too far away, since maybe there's a working faucet there. Then the memory of decay and desolation and the prospect of snakes and a clogged toilet spurs me after Ernie.

He's in better shape than I would have expected, matching me step for step for maybe 5 miles before we see a farmhouse in the distance.

"We can work for our supper," I say, starting to jog.

"What do you know about farming?" He jogs alongside me.

"More than I want to." Tending the gardens at East Wind is one of the better chores, after clerical stuff like checking out library books and issuing hall passes.

"More than I do, then."

At the house there's newspapers spilling out of the rural mail box. No lights. No car. Only a garage, where we'll be spending the night. A night without food, and after a brief inspection inside, one without even a dog bed or old mattress waiting for trash pick up.

"Well, at least I won't have to listen to Hoodoo's mouth." Ernie finds a dusty tarp and shakes out any spiders or other crawlies. He spreads it on the dirt floor. "And this is softer than concrete."

"Grass would be softer."

"Inside is safer."

I make a trip to the outside spigot and get a long drink of metallic-tasting water. "If it kills me," I quip, "At least I'll be out of my misery."

"We'll be okay," Ernie says just before the twilight turns to night.

"Sure we will," I answer, glad that dirt is softer than concrete. But not by much.

Sometime later, voices wake me. I can tell by Ernie's tense arm against mine that he's awake too. His fingers close on my wrist to keep me quiet. We listen. Two men are just outside, and I hear one of them say,

"What went wrong?"

The other asks, "Don't you know? They're after you."

Episode 5

My fingers tense into a fist, and Ernie's grip on my arm tightens. 'They're after you,' hits close to home, reminds me I need to check my back trail more often. The voices in the dark outside the doorway continue and I listen.

First man. "I thought he'd miss a bundle like this."

Second man. "Not him. The police. They think you did it."

A silence. I can feel the stunning blow those words gave somebody, and I wonder who he is. Somehow his voice sounds familiar and I listen harder. But the second voice keeps talking.

"I already took my share. It's the last you'll see of me. You best clear out too."

38

Wow, a bank robbery. A thrill of excitement and fear makes me shiver.

"How do you know? You didn't happen to leave anything for them to find, did you?"

That has a threatening edge, but the voice is still familiar. I punch my brain in an effort to remember who I've heard in the last few days besides Ernie's hipsie friends. A live person, not on tv. Not Al. Not the cafe lady. Not the bus driver. Who else?

Second man. "I never leave evidence. If I meant to hang you, would I be warning you?"

"Sorry. I'm just on edge. Helluva way to learn a thing like that."

"You know they always suspect the husband, John."

John goes on like he's telling himself the story. "Jordan must have thought she took the money. He lost his temper and she ended up dead." His anger spills over into the words. "He's the bastard who ought to pay. And he will."

Finally it hits me. In the cafe. Yesterday morning. The Actor. "Turn that up," he'd said, glued to the tv report on the mystery woman pulled from the well in Hackett. I remember thinking he knew who she was and would call the number on the screen. I must have heard him order breakfast earlier, but paid no attention, my mind being on how to get to Dentonville. My only goal, until I discovered I'd lost my traveling money. Now I have no goal except to stay away from East Wind as long as I can.

The other man says, "You need a good alibi. What will you p — " The pop of a fist hitting flesh, just like when Hoodoo hit Ernie, and a scuffle on the ground outside.

"Stop John I didn't mean — " Another blow. John says, "Keep your damn mouth shut."

Footsteps walk down the gravel drive. In a minute, a second set follows. A car engine sounds. Then another. Lights flash around as the cars depart, in different directions.

Ernie lets out a long breath, like he's been holding it. "Inside was safer." He lights up his watch dial. "Four o'clock."

39

"I don't think I can sleep any more," I tell him. "Maybe we should walk while it's cool." Hunger drives me. I remember the ten dollars the cafe lady gave me and can hardly wait to find a diner or cafe or town.

By dawn we've come to the end of the farm road and to a small bit of civilization pretty much like the one we left behind. A neon sign promises breakfast 24 hours and cheap prices. Ernie's eyes rove over a few cars parked under the streetlights. "Guess they're long gone."

"Franny and Hoodoo, or the bank robbers?"

"Those guys didn't rob a bank. Unless Jordan robbed it first."

We go inside, sit on stools at the counter. I have a moment of deja-vu before the waitress comes over. But there's no Actor/John. The only other customers are some blue-collar types, and one single mother with two little kids.

Ernie looks at the menu like he's never seen one before. He finally orders the ham and cheese omelet and hot tea. I'm surprised they have tea, and that he wants it. I leave off the bacon and coffee. Two fried eggs and a large orange juice, with a side of home fries. She brings enough for an army, so I'm looking at lunch too.

"Omigod," Ernie says, half standing up.

"What?!" I look everywhere, not knowing who he sees or what to expect.

"We can't pay for this."

"Relax. I can."

He gazes at me like I've grown another head.

"And have maybe a couple bucks left over." I give him a smile, then gulp half the orange juice. He sits down slowly, doubtful, and eats everything on his plate without another comment.

While he's thinking, so am I. Do I dare risk taking a 'bird bath' in the rest room, or should I just wash out my clothes? They'll dry on me soon enough under the June sun. Losing my toothbrush, toothpaste, and comb in the backpack Hoodoo drove away with means we have to hit a drug store next.

40

"Let's see if we can work off the breakfast," I suggest. "That way, we can spend my money on other stuff." I need sunglasses and a hat, too, but a couple bucks won't stretch to cover those luxuries. At least I don't need the jacket. I'm already sweating.

Ernie looks at me. "How much do you have?"

"Ten dollars."

He smiles like an indulgent uncle. I can see why Franny called him 'old man.'

"What's funny?"

"You," he says. Drains his tea. Then, "Work," he muses softly, like it's an unusual idea.

The waitress gives us the same look before she says, "Sure. The guy who sweeps is out sick with pink eye, and the window washer quit last week."

She shows us where the cleaners and carpet sweeper are kept, and I hand a pail and squeegee to Ernie. He stands holding them, looking helpless. For a moment it's like I'm seeing Al, blindly calling his dog, but the flash of fear and resentment comes and goes like summer lightning. "If you want to run the sweeper, I'll tackle the windows."

Ernie trades the tools and we work for almost an hour. The breakfast crowd has left and the lunch crowd hasn't started yet. If you could call the morning customers a crowd. I'm swiping down the last plate glass corner when something outside catches my eye. "Omigod." I sound like Ernie, only this time the stab of surprise has hit me.

He's on the other side of the room, trying to pick up biscuit crumbs with a sweeper chock full of trash. I run to him and point to a stocky broad-shouldered man on the pavement. Reading the menu. Bound to come in. "It's him!"

"Who?"

"John!"

He leans away, makes a skeptical face like he thinks I'm playing a joke on him. "You never saw him. What makes you so sure?"

"I did see him. Not last night. The morning before. In a cafe. The report on the tv shook him up. I heard his voice, and it's him. What'll we do?"

Ernie stares through the sparkling clean glass at the man I called Actor, whose voice belongs to John. "You're right about one thing. He is coming in."

The door opens and the waitress looks up. From her manner, all business-like, she's never seen him before. He sits on the end stool, just like in the other eatery, and she offers him the day's lunch special menu. He ignores it.

"Just coffee. Got any donuts?"

She lifts a dome lid off a pastry tray and sets the tray in front of him. He points to a couple and she uses tongs to lay them on a dessert plate. Goes to get the coffee.

"All done," Ernie tells her on the way to the back, and she nods. We stow the cleaning stuff and he hurries me through the exit into the alley. Full of food, smelly from cleaners, and without a clue what comes next.

"Shouldn't we call the police?" It's all I can do not to dance around like a nervous girl.

"Why? From what we heard, Jordan is the guilty guy."

"Husbands are almost always the killer."

"You watch too much television." Ernie follows the alley, not to the street but to the back parking lot.

Following Ernie, I'm about to mention my disappointment at not getting to wash myself or my clothes, when a parked car knocks me for a loop.

It's nestled between two large ornamental bushes, off the pavement and on the scraggly grass, like it's hiding.

Ernie lets out a low, long whistle of pure appreciation. He trots over to a pale pink Cadillac that's older than both of us put together. The bottom panel is black. Chrome so shiny it's a good thing the sun doesn't hit it or I'd be blinded without any sunglasses.

"Let's find a drug store," I say. It's the first time in my life my teeth haven't been brushed for three days straight. "And then a

42

thrift store." If I can't wash my clothes, I can buy clean second hand jeans and a couple of tee-shirts.

"Take my picture," Ernie says, leaning against the car and smiling.

"What?"

"Take my picture. Or doesn't your camera work?"

"It works." Sliding the camera from my hip pocket, where it kept out of the way while I washed the windows, I hope it does. Ernie's face is so eager and happy, I snap a couple.

He tries the door. Locked of course. The interior is show room clean. I can tell he yearns to sit behind the wheel. "That waitress can't afford this antique."

He shakes his head. "No. It belongs to John."

Terror rips through me. The car is hiding, all right. Just like it was in the back lot of the Morningbird Hotel the night of the storm, when I woke and fled from that ghostly, inhuman wailing. Was it a grief so deep I'd never felt anything like it, or an anger so violent that I dreaded imagining its source?

Grabbing Ernie's arm, I pull him along. We race over the curb and across the grass to the next street. He doesn't ask me what's wrong. I guess he can figure that out. Luck on my side, there's a drug store. We go in and I pick up a small plastic basket, which I load with the stuff I need. He stands with his hands braced on his hipbones, staring toward the diner, seeing that Caddy only in his dreams.

When we're back on the sidewalk, my disguise hat and dark glasses in place, I glance about for a secondhand shop that doesn't have all dresses displayed in the window. Two blocks over, we find one. I buy a duffel bag for fifty cents, and pack two dollars' worth of traveling clothes inside. Ernie's content to travel in his expensive duds even if they are starting to smell. I pick up a used deodorant for a dime and toss it to him. "Thanks," he says.

Using my last dollar, I pick out a nice striped shirt and a pair of jeans that I think will fit him. Stuff them into my duffel bag. He'll be glad to wear them before long.

"What next, boss?" I ask, feeling light as air and ready for anything.

"You're not tired of all this? Don't want to go home?"

"Do you?" Wherever his home is, it's probably a nice brick with a big yard and maybe a white fence to keep out neighbor dogs. But he's on a mission, and I'm curious about how he plans to carry it out. Chasing Hoodoo and Franny is okay but catching them seems as unlikely as stealing John's car and taking a joy ride.

He sits down on a shaded bench in front of the thrift store. "You forgot the take out carton with the leftover fries."

Yeah, I did.

"We could go back, see if she's thrown them out."

"I'm not going back there."

"He's probably finished eating and is on his way to Canada."

"Sure he is. If that's where Jordan went. You heard him. He's gonna make Jordan pay. Maybe he did kill her, and wants to pin the murder on Jordan."

"And maybe he's just out for revenge." Ernie shifts restlessly on the bench. His teeth are too clean for him to be a smoker, but I bet he'd like to have a pack and lighter right now, something to distract his thoughts and calm his nerves.

"Root beer does it for me," I say.

"What?"

"Distracts my thoughts and calms my nerves."

Ernie laughs shortly. "You're a funny kid."

When we walk back to the parking lot, the Caddy is gone. Tire tracks lead into the grove of trees behind the diner and out on a side street. Ernie heaves a sigh. "At least I'll have a picture.

He uses the cafe phone to cancel the credit card. I ask the waitress about the fries. She takes a little white bag out of a cooler. Tosses in a couple of cans of cola. I almost ask for root beer instead but thank her and carry my duffel bag out to where Ernie's sitting on another bench, watching squirrels in the trees across the street. We share the fries, washing them down with the drinks. "You haven't asked me a single question."

44

"Yes I did. I asked if you wanted some grape juice. Then I asked why you can't go home. If you have a deadline. And if you're happy. You said you were. Past tense. And when I asked what happened, you didn't answer. But I can see that you are. The rest doesn't matter."

"Phenomenal." I'm impressed that he remembers all this. I hadn't realized I was being questioned, or that I'd answered. "You're one sharp dude."

This time he laughs so hard he loses his breath. "Then what the hell am I doing out here?"

"You're on a mission. You want to save Francine from Hoodoo. And I'm here to help you."

"Some missions fail, no matter who helps."

I gather up our trash and stuff it into a bin, feeling guilty that the aluminum cans should be recycled.

I wonder where we'll spend tonight, and what we'll do with the hours in between, besides work for food and use public rest rooms. If I hadn't spent all my money, we could find a Laundromat and have a clean change for later. If I were at East Wind, I'd be in the library, draped in my favorite wing chair, reading the end of that bookshop mystery. Tall windows let in cool breezes that carry whiffs from the cafeteria, hinting of lunch. If . . . .

"They're here!"

Ernie's excitement startles me, but not as much as his hands roughly pushing me around the corner of the building. "Who?"

He flattens himself against the bricks, one arm shielding me beside him like a mama protecting her kid, and I freak. Collins has somehow managed to trail me and the cops are coming with billy sticks and handcuffs.

Some missions fail. The humiliation of being that failure propels me down the alley. Ernie races after and catches me by the wrist. "What're you doing? I don't want to lose them again."

He drags me back toward the street, where the SUV has stopped for a red light.

Episode 6

Ernie charges toward the SUV like he thinks he's going to catch it. I shoulder my duffel bag and chase after him, but the light changes and the SUV moves on into the next block. I stop. Ernie doesn't.

If the next light turns in our favor, there's a chance he might make it to the door in time to— Do what? Jump in? Haul Franny out? I take off running again, to be there when whatever's going to happen, happens.

Morning traffic is heavier now, but it's a small town, few people on the sidewalks. One of the storefronts I pass proves to be a Laundromat. At the end of the block the light is still green and the SUV skims through it and away down a long hill toward an Interstate ramp.

Catching up to Ernie, I want to say 'Give it up, pal.' Head back to Main Street and bum enough coins to do our laundry. Brush my teeth at the sink while the machines are churning. He has other ideas. "Come on!" He's spotted a cab stand.

A middle-aged driver sits in his cab, reading a newspaper. Looks up when Ernie snatches open the back door and we pile in. His eyes in the rearview don't come across as friendly. "Where to?"

"See that blue SUV going up the ramp? Follow it."

The cab motor doesn't start on the first try, and Ernie's impatience shows in every tense line of his body. When we're moving, he sags in relief. We're two cars behind the SUV on the Interstate. I wonder where they're going. What we'll do when they get there. How we'll pay the driver.

Ahead, Hoodoo pulls off only a few exits later, at a rest area.

"There is a God," Ernie says softly.

Our cabbie signals a lane change and takes us to the edge of the parking lot, where cars go one way and trucks veer off to a larger space. Ernie's door is open before the brakes finish, and the cab driver yells, "Hold on, bub! You gotta pay."

"Wait—"

"Pay now or I call the cops."

Ernie rips a silvery necklace over his head. "Here!" The clasp is one of those magnet types, and he slides off a small medallion before dropping the chain on the front seat.

He's gone, but the cabbie holds up the chain with a greedy surprised look that prompts me to grab it out of his hand. "Not that." Fumbling in haste, I eject the cartridge from my camera and toss the camera over to him. "Three exits' worth." I slam the cab door. His tires screech angrily half way across the trucker's lot.

It's an old rest area and the untrimmed bushes lining the walk make good cover. As soon as I join Ernie behind one, he says, "Watch the doors and whistle when one of them comes out."

About 5 spaces farther on, the SUV stands head and shoulders above lesser cars. Curtains are open and I glimpse Ernie inside. Either he has a key, or one of them left it unlocked. Then I concentrate on watching the rest room doors. Some traveler puts coins in a drink machine and the can clunks into the tray. A car pulls out. Birds twitter in a tree nearby.

The men's side is nearer me. I wish Ernie would come back but since I don't know if he's coming back, my palms start to sweat and spit dries up in my mouth. Then Hoodoo steps into view in the lobby area and I try to whistle. Useless.

Dodging along the row of cars, I reach the back door of the SUV just as Ernie jumps out almost on top of me. He's carrying a gray blanket wadded into a bundle and sweat has made spikes of hair stick to his forehead. Hunkered, we hurry away from the scene of the crime and crouch down on the far side of a silver Lexus.

I pop up for an instant and see Hoodoo outside the lobby, kicking at an acorn on the walkway, smoking.

"What'd you find?" I nod toward the gray bundle.

Ernie doesn't answer. He's looking up at a sturdy white haired lady who's come up to the car and stands motionless like she's about to step on two snakes.

"Harold." Her voice holds a quiet but stricken warning.

From the driver's side of the Lexus, Harold answers, "What?"

"Don't unlock the car. There might be a b—"

His key clicks, he opens the door, there's the clack of her door unlocking and the power window rolls down. His tone is peevish. "What's the matter with you?"

At that moment something small escapes Ernie's wadded blanket and hits the asphalt like a pigmy bomb. The woman leaps a foot into the air and squeals. Harold's voice demands, "What the hell's the matter? Get in."

Ernie's hand shoots out and retrieves a brown pill bottle. The woman cries, "Lock the door Harold!"

She can't get in because we're blocking her door. She's still standing, barely, knees trembling. It's too pathetic to be funny, yet laughter bubbles up and when I glance at Ernie he's holding it in, too, like when Steve got the giggles in chapel and we all ended up in D-hall for three days. Snickering like fools, Ernie and I scoot away from her car and stagger across the road into the safety of another bush and collapse.

We're heaving deep breaths when the Lexus rolls by us and down the slope toward the Interstate. The woman's putting on her seat belt. I can almost hear Harold cussing. I feel sorry we gave her such a fright. Then the whole thing flashes like a double-time commercial and it's funny again. The way she couldn't move. The way he not only unlocked the door but put the key in the ignition and unlocked hers. And rolled down her window and yelled at her like everything was her fault.

Then it isn't funny. She will forever believe we're druggies. Car thieves. Terrorists. And clueless Harold who didn't see us will never believe she did. I keep snickering. Nerves I guess.

"Shhh!" Ernie draws his legs in, backing into the bush, and I do the same.

Doors slam, and the SUV zooms past toward the Interstate.

They've been gone at least two minutes before Ernie crawls out of the bush with the bundle and squats on the grass. His hands are shaking when he unfolds part of the blanket. A plastic grocery bag full of prescription pill bottles spills over. "No wonder he's crazy," I say.

"Oh, he doesn't take them all. Just maybe half."

"And sells the rest."

"You got it."

"We won't do that, will we?"

Ernie's glance is sharp enough to cut. "Of course not." He wrestles with the loose ends of the blanket, picks it up. We go toward the Men's.

"Why didn't we take the wheels? You have a key."

"I have a duplicate door key. Hoodoo has the ignition."

"Oh." Too bad. Riding in luxury for a change would be nice.

In the rest room Ernie goes into a stall and I hear bottles rattling against each other and pills dropping into the commode. Flush. More pills. Flush. He comes out, the bag looks full but half are empty containers. Goes into another stall. Repeats. When he comes out this time with the gray blanket, it's a neat sausage shape, a cowboy's bedroll. There's still something inside, bulging the middle like an egg in a snake.

That makes me laugh again, imagining the woman in the parking lot telling her friends about the two drug dealers who almost stole their Lexus.

Ernie's face stops me mid-chuckle. "Let me have your belt."

I unbuckle it and he uses it to strap the ends of the bedroll so whatever's in there won't fall out. "What is that?"

"Hoodoo's gun."

"Hoodoo had a gun?" A mixture of fear and awe tips my stomach but doesn't turn it over. I feel lucky he didn't at some point shoot one of us, and pride in Ernie for stealing it out of the SUV without getting caught.

"You didn't find your credit card?"

"No. I'd have to pick Hoodoo's pocket."

We're too far away now to go back to that Laundromat, but I can hear old Collie's voice prodding me, "Cleanliness is next to Godliness." I've discovered that three days of sweat is my limit, not to mention that little accident when Hoodoo decked Ernie.

And to keep the dentist away from my teeth, I'm determined to clean up while the means are available.

"Watch the door," I say, and Ernie meanders to the entrance while I strip down and fill a sink with hand soap and hot water. In go the whites. I let them soak while the next sink fills with warm rinse water.

When I'm finished, jeans teeth hair and all, and wearing the thrift store outfit, I'm stuck with wet clothes and don't know what to do with them. The hot air hand dryer would take all day, even if it worked.

"Your turn," I tell Ernie. He gets up from the doorway like he's a hundred years old. I take his place beside the bedroll, and wave away a twenty-something who looks like he needs to go right now. He moves on to another Men's farther along. Ernie says behind me, "What are these?"

I know what he means but glance around to see his expression. He's holding up the clothes I bought for him. "Yours. Think they'll fit?"

"Yeah," he answers and goes off to take his bath and change. I hear him filling sinks and sloshing his dirty clothes, and when he gets to the shampoo part he actually whistles a tuneless tune.

I envy him his expensive running shoes. My sneaker soles feel as thin as a mouse pad. "Mouse," I say softly, missing the computer in the library, even if it does have a zillion kid controls imposed by old Collie.

"Mouse?"

Ernie's wet hair is slicked back off his face, like he's just climbed out of the East Wind swimming pool. Even in faded jeans and t-shirt he still has the slumming executive look that I've come to know. I realize he'll never be one of us. 'Us' meaning the underdog-waiting-for-a-break with a mandatory sentence of three-to-five ahead of him. I don't know where I'm going from here, but it's sure not back there.

"Ready to roll?" I stand up. "Man, I'm hungry!"

Ernie laughs. "You sound like Fran."

Then he holds up his dripping upscale shirt. "I hate to throw this away, but the tag says 'Dry Clean Only' and wringing it out will finish ruining it."

"You wrung out the pants. Go ahead. Make them match."

A pained frown before he laughs again. "What the hell." He twists the shirt tail and a pint of water flows out into a floor drain. Holding it by the shoulders, he snaps it a few times, then lays it over his arm on top of the pants.

I remember his necklace and take it from my pocket. "Here. This might make you feel better."

He picks the double-linked chain off my palm as if it's treasure from the Atocha. "How'd you get this?"

"Trade," I answer, watching him replace the medallion and anchor the magnets around his neck. He picks up the bulky bedroll.

"Traded what?"

I pick up my duffel bag. "My camera."

His mouth flies open to protest but I show him the film cartridge and we step out into the summer sunshine as happy as if we had good sense. That's what Steve claims his grandma used to say, before she died and his parents split up and put him in custodial care. I wonder if my parents are alive or dead, remarried with new families or pushing up daisies.

Collins had made it clear he couldn't — or wouldn't — answer questions like that. Clear too that I was NEVER to ask anybody in the couple of foster homes I'd been in when I was little. I try hard, not for the first time, to remember a grandma or other relatives, but the blurry faces I used to think I remembered have gone the way of the voices, which I can't hear anymore.

I check the drink machines and find enough coins to buy one can. Ernie and I spread our wet clothes on a picnic table, then sit on the shaded bench and share the drink. We watch rest stop patrons come and go. After a while, the parking spaces are empty. Birds have gone deeper into the woods in the noon heat and travelers are sitting in air-conditioned cafes chowing down on salads and burgers. "What day is it?"

"Damned if I know. Thursday?"

No school, no tv, no schedule, no plan. What day it is no longer matters. I stretch my legs out in front of me and lean back against the picnic table. Aluminum snap crackle pops as Ernie squashes the empty can. He lobs it into the wire bin ten feet away.

Then a blonde girl about Ernie's age drives up in a screaming red sports car.

Episode 7

Well, not a sports car, but a sporty one, a convertible. And the top's down. Daddy's girl with her first wheels, the kind Jerry's always talking about. As if he'd ever been near either one.

Ernie doesn't show a lot of interest until she finishes checking her hair and lipstick in the rear view mirror and swings long tanned legs out of the car. Her white dress is too small, not because she's fat but because she bought it that way, and the heeled sandals make her teeter towards us.

"Hello." She takes off oversized sun glasses. She's speaking to him, acts like she doesn't see me right beside him.

"Hello," Ernie answers, and I can't tell anything from his tone. He does sit up, though, crossing his ankles and resting his arms on his knees.

"Is this a private party, or can anybody play?"

"It's a public place. Pull up a chair."

"Cute kid," she says, still watching him.

Ernie answers, "Not mine!"

She laughs and points at me. Then I remember that's what my thrift store t-shirt says on the chest. Cute kid. It should say Mouse.

A toss of her head flips her long hair back and forth. "I've never seen either of you cuties around here before. You guys brothers?"

Together we answer. I say "Yes" he says "No" and she gives us an amused look.

"Which one of you is clueless?"

We point at each other. "He is."

She laughs again. "You could take this act on the road." There's about two seconds of silence before she adds, "Wanna ride?"

"Sure," Ernie says and I nearly fall off the picnic table.

"Back in a sec." She goes toward the Ladies' side of the building.

Ernie starts folding our dry clothes. I help, and we pack our bags.

When we're in her car — me in the back with the duffel and blanket — I want to ask where we're going but she floors the gas pedal and I'm jerked breathless. Her hair flies in the wind, and she's talking to Ernie and he's answering but I can't catch the words. His hand clenches the console as if he might be regretting this decision already.

We fly along the Interstate until we pass a speed limit sign and she slows down. I start to breathe again. By the time I'm relaxed enough to enjoy the ride, we're many exits from the rest area and she signals a turn. At the top of the ramp there's signs for everything, including food. I like her better now.

We end up at some little Italian restaurant that promises a meal anytime, day or night. I'm ready for spaghetti and garlic bread. The smells filling the place remind me of Friday nights when Collins would take a bus load of us to Nikky's Ristorante in Hackett. It had to be somebody's birthday, and Nikky would come to the table and sing a sappy song in Italian to the Happy Birthday tune.

She puts the car top up and we go inside. Fancier than anything I'm used to, with table cloths and a space for a dance floor. There are booths and we have our choice of seating.

Nobody else is eating pasta at five in the afternoon, and the waiter must have gone home or is in the back washing dishes. We munch on breadsticks for what feels like an hour.

The blonde is older than I first thought, twenty-five or more, and she's sitting so close to Ernie, what she's saying reaches his ears but not mine. Her hand keeps straying to his necklace. Strokes it like a pet pooch. If she's laying on the lovey-dovey talk, I don't really care to listen. Can't tell how Ernie's taking it. She probably can't, either.

Finally a waiter writes up our order. He brings a large green bottle of some red wine. She studies the label, tips the guy with a smile, and he fills a glass each for her and Ernie. They sniff and sip like they know what they're doing.

It's another long time before the waiter brings a tray loaded with small salads and dishes of pasta. The meatballs are tender and tasty, so I leave off wondering what's going on in my dorm, or what will happen later tonight. Somewhere soft music plays, and Ernie and his new friend leave stuff on their plates and go off to dance.

The salt and spices made me thirsty, so I finish my soft drink and fill the glass from the wine bottle. Steve used to have an uncle who got drunk every Friday night, to dull his pain. Right now, with a belly stuffed with spaghetti, garlic bread, and cola, I don't have any pain, just curiosity. I sniff and sip, and it's not bad. Grape juice with a bite.

Before the music stops and the dancing comes to a halt, I've drunk half a bottle and am feeling fine.

They come back to cold food. She sends Ernie to find the waiter, who takes the plates away, returns them steaming from a microwave. "Any dessert?" he asks me.

"Go ahead," she urges. "They have a coconut pie to die for."

Coconut pie, who can resist that? It's one of my favorites, and she's paying. At least, I hope she is.

The pie's fresh and the slice is huge. The first few bites are delicious but I find myself forcing the rest on top of everything else in my stomach. Their quiet voices pick up where they left off, and her laughter tells me she's enjoying Ernie's company more than her warmed-over lasagna. An afternoon rainstorm blows in, darkening the place.

The waiter lights some candles and places them on the next table. The distant yearning music starts again, their desserts are on the way, and suddenly I'm so sleepy I can't keep my eyes open.

I'm jostled awake just enough to realize Ernie's picking me up off the booth seat. The woman says, "Your bro's okay. It's a quality wine."

"He's underage," Ernie answers, sounding pissed.

"Shhhhhhh!" She giggles. "How was I to know he'd guzzle it down like a little wino?"

"Give me the keys. I'll carry him out."

"I can walk," I say, the words leaving my mouth on little bird wings and flying ahead of me. I'm flying too, in the candlelit music, right out the door and into the threatening storm.

Ernie lays me on the back seat and I think I'm asleep and dreaming. Like that night at the Morningbird. I wonder what a morning bird is. Does it cry and moan? Maybe it's a mourning bird, and that's the sound I heard. Not John at all. But birds don't drive big bulky antique cars. Or sleek red sporty cars.

"Think he'll tell your father?"

There's a pause. "No. But he won't feel too good when he wakes up."

"That won't be for a while."

Lightning flashes in the rain-dark sky. Or is it night? The car has stopped. The world keeps going around and I figure I'd better not try to sit up. Opening my eyes, I can see them in the front. She's got Ernie scrunched against the passenger door, but he's not making any moves.

"I bought the meal." She sounds peevish.

"Thank you." Ernie answers like he doesn't know she's mad, but I'm not fooled. He knows, doesn't care.

"Did you think I wouldn't want anything in return? I pay, you pay."

"Not like that."

"Why not? Afraid I'll give you a disease?"

Mouse lies still, hoping they don't realize I'm awake and listening. But when Ernie tells her, "I've made a rule not to have sex with anybody I haven't known at least a month," I snicker.

She thinks he's joking, since she says in a sweeter tone, "I can't wait that long. Can you?" She leans into him, and in a panicked voice he yells, "Vinnie! Unlock the door!"

Swaying like the drunken kid that I am, I leap up and pop the master door lock on the driver's side. She screams, "Get out then! Get out of my car and take the little bastard with you!"

Ernie's feet hit the ground before she finishes ranting.

He opens my door, hauls me out. Shoves my duffel bag into my arms and snatches up the blanket bed roll. My head spins and my knees buckle but I manage not to collapse. She starts the engine, guns it, and the car leaps away so powerfully that the open doors slam shut.

We watch her tail lights disappear down a lonely back road. Summer lightning still flickers about the evening sky. I'm standing in a rain-filled pot hole. "Where are we?"

Now Ernie sounds peevish. "About ten miles from the restaurant. At least twenty from that rest area. And a helluva long way from the last town."

"Ten miles. Piece of cake." I stagger toward the side of the road, and am grateful when Ernie steers me back onto the asphalt. Thunder in the distance. Lightning. Dark clouds roll across the moonlit sky towards us. Feels later than it could possibly be.

Far down the straightaway we see car lights coming back. "Think that's her?"

He shoves me across the ditch and into waist-high weeds, where we crouch until the car zooms by. "Guess it was."

"Sorry we didn't let her pick us up again?"

We walk along the dark road for maybe a hundred yards before he answers. "No."

Another hundred yards. "You heard me snicker, didn't you."

"I'm glad you were alert enough to pop that lock."

Another hundred yards. "Um. If you didn't want to boink her, what did you two do for the last three hours?"

"Told each other lies."

"Tell them to me."

"Like a bedtime story?" Humor has crept back into his voice.

"Yeah, I —" Another pot hole. Except this one throws me. Knees and arms catch the impact, my face hits as an afterthought.

Ernie picks me up. "Are you all right?"

Now I do have a pain, like my brain's two sizes too big and the world's spinning again. I want to sit down but that would be wimpy. "Never felt better."

"I bet."

A mile or so ahead, a security light guards a construction site. Thunder's closer now, and I smell rain coming. Near the chain link fence, sections of a huge drainage system wait to be installed. It reminds me of the fence at East Wind and right now I'd trade my comic book collection to be safe inside those familiar brick walls. Or at least inside one of these giant pipes, shelter from the storm. Ernie reads my mind, because he asks, "How good are you at climbing?"

"Drunk or sober?"

"How drunk are you?"

"Not enough to try climbing over that fence. I did that at East Wind, and see where it got me."

"I thought you loved the life of the open road."

"Sometimes I guess I do. Not when I'm about to be struck by lightning."

Wind rolls in tree-shaking gusts over us, bringing the downpour. "We're more likely to drown if we stand here." Ernie starts running down a side road. With no other plan, I stumble along after him, dizzy, wet, cold, and queasy from undigested stuff like a rock in my gut.

We leave the construction site behind. Soon I don't see its light anymore. We pass through a blind space, trusting the asphalt beneath our feet to keep us moving. Presently, little lights mark a utility outpost, a roadside stand locked up for the night, and a small used car lot. Ernie halts in front of me so suddenly that I bang into him.

"Sanctuary," he tells me.

"You've found a church?" Shivering, my teeth chattering, I long for quiet, dry, candlelit. Peering into the darkness ahead of us, I see a large old brick building. Tall windows glisten from a flickering flood light which shines on a sign that reads 'Haw Creek Elementary School.'

I groan. "Not another school."

Ernie searches in the weeds, finds a bottle, draws back to throw. I grab his arm, screeching, "East Wind has a burglar — "

It's the wrong arm and he completes the throw. The bottle crashes through a bottom window, breaking out several panes and the thin rotten wood strips that held them in place. " — alarm." If I weren't so sick and tired, I'd flee the scene before the cops arrive, but I am sick, and tired, and my head's throbbing. My nose, knees, and arms burn from the fall on the asphalt earlier.

Nothing happens. No one comes. No sirens, twirling lights, uniforms or handcuffs.

Ernie takes Hoodoo's gun from the bed roll and knocks off the shards of glass with the barrel. Half expecting the gun to fire and give us both a heart attack, I'm actually relieved when he says, "Come on. I'll boost you up."

We land in a classroom dimly lit by a distant street lamp. Fourth grade artwork is taped around the walls. We move between rows of desks toward an open hall door. We're nearly there when Ernie rushes me into a closet where we cower. I'm glad there are no wire hangers to clatter. Something squishy is underfoot but I'm more worried by the heavy footsteps coming into the room. A flashlight darts around but doesn't spot us behind the louvers.

As the night watchman moves down the aisle toward the broken window, I hear him mutter, "Damn vandals." He picks up the bottle and tosses it into a metal waste basket. The loud bang zings through my head like a bullet and almost makes me throw up.

He goes out and shuts the door. I listen hard to see if he locks it, but the drumming between my ears is too loud. We wait in the closet until I think I'll smother. Then we wait in the classroom, standing ready to hide again in case the old guy comes back.

I'm dozing against Ernie's shoulder when he whispers, "Think he holes up in the infirmary?"

"Nah, it's probably locked to keep the drugs from escaping."

"You're a witty dude, you know that?" He cautiously opens the door and we wait some more. I'm not cold now, and the draft from the broken window feels good on my face. He continues, "Then, if we break in there, he's not likely to find us."

"You looking for a fix? You won't find much. Twelve percent cough syrup, tops."

"If I wanted a fix, I'd've kept Hoodoo's stash. A cot, and maybe another blanket."

"I could go for that."

The long hallway is backlit through a row of rain-patterned windows. I wonder if there's a town nearby, and by morning I'll be ready for the prospect of breakfast without strings attached. What really kept Ernie from having a fling with that blonde? Her age? The lame excuse he gave her? The fact that I was with them, and awake?

We pass a closed door that has a brass sign bolted on. TEACHERS LOUNGE. Light shows beneath it, and inside a radio plays low. Sounds like 'A Prairie Home Companion' and I'd like to stop and listen but Ernie keeps going until there's another brass sign. INFIRMARY.

He lays down the bed roll, limp because he's carrying Hoodoo's gun in his waistband. Tries the door. Uses his pocket knife to jimmy the lock.

"You're good at this, you know. Breaking and entering."

"I'm good at a lot of things," he tells me, and then we're inside the windowless room. Before he closes the door behind us, I get a glimpse of shelves, cabinets, and a desk.

Episode 8

No sound, except our breathing. The space reeks of industrial strength disinfectant. Behind me, Ernie stuffs our blanket under the door and I imagine us suffocating in our sleep. A faint grayness fills a wide doorway, so there must be another room with a window. I start forward to open it. Stumbling into a desk, I bang my already bruised knee.

Then light shoots into my eyes and bounces around inside my head. "Ow! That's bright."

"Keep your voice down." Ernie goes to the shelves where boxes of bandages and other medical stuff sit alongside a clutter of lost and found items.

Limping, I pass a sink and a rest room stall in a cubbyhole between the dispensary and the infirmary. This room is like a barracks, three army cots with sheets and pillows without cases. The window opens easily, and I draw in long breaths of rain-cool air. There's an old metal screen. No bars.

When I return to Ernie he's prying at the lock on an upper cabinet. I tell him what I've found. He warns me, "If you use the toilet, don't flush." Sounds like he's had a taste of community living, too, with plumbing that talks. I try to guess whether it's boarding or military prep. He looks too young for college.

"If there's any pain killer, I could use some of that."

"I thought you never felt better."

"I lied." Almost every part of me aches or stings for one reason or another.

"You'll feel worse in the morning." The lock snaps and the cabinet doors swing open. He picks a small bottle of children's aspirin and tosses it to me.

"This stuff is dangerous," I say, and pop half a dozen into my mouth. The orange flavor brings memories of being sick and helpless. Chewing them would make me gag, so I head for the sink.

"Want a cup?" He holds up a plastic tumbler.

And risk every kiddy germ known to man? "Unnn-unnn."

When I lean over to catch the water in my mouth, it washes the tablets right down the drain. I stagger toward him, giggling.

Ernie's reaching for something at the back of the second cabinet, which he's just broken into. He gives me a one-sided smile. "You're still drunk."

"Yeah, I must be." I wheel out the desk chair and make myself comfortable.

As he liberates a thin stack of comic books, a small white sandal falls on his foot. He bends, picks it up, turns it this way and that. It looks slightly familiar to me but I don't have any reason to recognize a single shoe belonging to a fourth grade girl.

That doesn't stop my mouth. "I bet I know where that came from. A one-legged midget lost it on the playground when she was running to catch her bus, and a teacher found it and put it there in nineteen-forty-seven." That's the date carved into the front of this building. "The bus wrecked and everyone was killed and nobody thought about the shoe ever again."

He lays it on the cabinet shelf. "Francine had a pair like this when she was nine. She used to carry around a story book called 'Dependable Fran' and try to make me read it to her."

His voice breaks on the last few words, and I'm sorry for making a crummy joke. The shoe is familiar : Fran was wearing white sandals in that picnic park, when I first saw her. "Give me some more aspirin."

"You've had enough."

The giggles bubble up and I clamp my hand over my mouth, though I'm pretty sure these walls are thicker than those at East

Wind and that night watchman's halfway down the hall from here.

"What's funny now?"

I don't tell him, but empty out another half dozen tablets. Toss them one by one like popcorn, trying to catch them in my mouth. They're heavier than popcorn, and my timing is way off. Ernie laughs and shakes his head as they roll across the floor like little live things. Then I catch one and chew it just enough to swallow. Somehow the aspirin bottle gets away from me and crashes into a tin wastebasket.

He leaps a foot in the air. "Help me move the desk," he says. We place it against the door. He's carrying Hoodoo's gun in his waistband again, since the bed roll is doing duty as a light blocker. He hits the switch anyway and we lean on the desk in the darkness, straining to hear footsteps. I don't believe he'll shoot even if the old man manages to push into the room. Nobody tries, so he turns the light on and we relax.

After changing into dry clothes, we sit around reading the boring assortment of comic books. 'Prairie Home Companion' must have finished its time slot. What follows? Maybe the watchman has changed the station, or gone to bed. I feel like I'm back at East Wind, with a new roommate.

"Wish I had a library book."

"Doesn't take much to make you happy, does it?"

"And a million dollars."

"I'll settle for a good night's sleep."

We take turns at the sink to brush our teeth. In the dimly lit mirror I can see the skinned place on my chin, another on my elbow. Ernie peers at my reflection. He lifts my other arm and inspects it. "Both of them."

He rummages in the dispensary cabinet and returns with a tin of pink ointment that smells sweet and old-fashioned. He smears it on the scrapes, and I can tell he's had experience doing this for Fran before they grew up.

"You're a great brother, Ernie," I say. "Wish I could come live with you when you go home."

He tenses. Hands me the salve tin. "Who says I'm ever going home?" Halfway into the barracks, he calls, "Switch off the light, will you?"

I drop my jeans and put ointment on my skinned knees. I can't remember what day tomorrow will be, but I ought to call Jerry or Steve, even if that sends me to D-hall for the rest of my life. Not knowing what's going on there is worse than not knowing where I'll be tomorrow night after dark.

He's lying on the farthest cot, arms over his face like a shield. I'm exhausted, too keyed-up to sleep. A strong cool breeze spatters light rain against the screen. He's restless, and I want to try to smooth over the stupid things I keep saying. "You're like me."

"Oh, yeah? How?" There's interest in his voice, like if he was mad earlier, he's not now.

"You always want to do the right thing."

"Like running away and carrying a concealed weapon and breaking into a kiddy school," he says, and I can feel him smiling.

"And letting that trashy girl get me drunk."

He laughs, so I know he knows I'm teasing. Thunder in the distance grows fainter. The storm is passing, only an occasional lightning flash to remind us. That, and the lingering wet-dust smell that follows.

Ernie's working the screen off the window when I wake.

Summer heat's coming in, promising a scorcher, and it's barely June. Or is it August? I've lost all sense of time and reality's rapidly leaving. The lumpy blanket and my duffel bag wait on his cot.

'My bags are packed and I'm ready to go' runs through my aching head, and the effort to come up with the next line threatens to split it in two. I wish I'd chewed those damned aspirin last night. If wine does this to me, I'll never drink anything stronger.

"What's the plan?" I suspect there isn't any, but I'm curious about what he'll say.

"Be long gone before the security guard starts patrolling."

Considering that we've breached most of the security here without getting caught, and that night watchman likely has gone home to breakfast, I leisurely perform as much of my morning ritual as these limited circumstances allow. Are the guys back in the dorm hovering near the pay phone in the lobby? Being grilled by old Collie, or worse, thrown in chains by O'Leary himself?

"Aghhh!" The screen twists out of Ernie's grasp and falls with a clatter to the ground below.

We freeze, him kneeling at the window sill, me just leaving the stall. By tonight, the smell in here is more likely to alert the old man than any noise.

"Let's go!" Ernie throws our gear out the window and straddles the window ledge.

The last thing I see is his hands gripping the weathered wood, and then he drops. I reach in and flush the john. As I'm ducking under the window frame, I hear the door knob rattle and a hoarse voice yells, "Come out of there, you little bastards. I've called the cops."

Fearful he has a gun and might shoot through the door, I let go. . .

. . . and land in an ankle-wrenching bed of pea gravel. Ernie shoves the duffel into my arms and I run after him, surprised to find myself on a hedged sidewalk, a canopy of old trees shaking hands over the roadway. It's a residential section, but I'm fleeing and can't pay attention to the houses except to sense they're middle-class or better, with gates and flowers and big trees. The kind of place I'd like to live one day.

The kind of place the counselor at East Wind once dangled like a candy bar in front of me so I'd eat my carrots and not cry at night. Well, I ate them and cried only in my nightmares. I decide not to call my brainless friends. Let them get what's coming to them.

Then I change my mind again. So what if Jerry wanted a good laugh? He did me a favor. The least I can do is return it. I'll call Collins and tell him the prank was all my idea. That I've

64

found a good home and not to expect me back or try to find me. It's a nice thought, anyway.

Ernie has slowed to a walk. Good thing we're not still running, because in another minute a Public Safety car with two guys in it sirens by at twice the speed limit.

I figure we're about eight blocks away from Haw Creek Elementary, safely minding our own business and in sight of civilization, when ahead the coughing of a lawnmower gives Ernie an idea. He jogs half a block and stops in a driveway.

"Need help?"

The man raises his head, peers at us. His face is blotched and sweat rolls down his red cheeks. "Damn thing won't start." He kicks a front tire. Tosses Ernie the pull cord. Stands back.

Instead of wearing himself out, Ernie tinkers with levers and switches, or whatever those things are that adjust stuff. Jerry would know. And cuss when nothing he did worked. Whatever Ernie does, works. One pull and the engine lets out a blast and starts to roar.

The man's face smooths into an almost-smile. I can't hear any words, but with their lips moving and gestures, Ernie settles some kind of deal. The man goes into his house, wiping his forehead and neck with a large dirty handkerchief. Ernie starts mowing the modest front lawn.

He's on the last lap when the man comes back out, swigging from a tall frosty glass. I expect money to exchange hands. Maybe I'll have an omelet with my orange juice.

He shuts off the engine and the scene turns ugly. The man's face is red again, this time with anger. "You said you'd cut the lawn. You'll get the price we agreed on when you're finished." He goes to a high wooden fence attached to his house and opens a gate. There's a back yard, a big one, enclosed in the same style.

For a moment I think Ernie might slug him, but he just stands there hands on his hips, thinking. Then he nods me to follow, and pushes the silent mower forward. I pick up our bedroll and duffel. Once we're in, the man closes the gate behind us.

"Did he lock it?"

"Don't know. Don't care." Ernie cranks the mower and walks it across the grass, cutting a wavy path. He kicks a back gate open, and we race through a dozen yards, stopping only when we no longer hear the engine.

So we're in another unfamiliar town, with no money. Back on a sidewalk, we pass a shady park bench. Squirrels are busy finding bits of food thrown down for them by nice people. "Stay here," I tell him.

His words "Where are you go — " trail after me.

I turn a corner and am in front of a jeweler's store. A dozen other businesses line this side, and across the street are their twins. Bonanza.

Leaving on my sunglasses, I hold my hat in front of me and enter a clean and brightly lit place where thick carpet mutes my steps. A bell tinkles my presence, but I'm at the counter a long minute before a young woman looks up from a stapled bunch of papers. "Can I help you?" she asks doubtfully.

"Yes, Ma'am, I think you can."

I abandoned my Scout-on-a-Hike story on the way in, so fly by my shirt tail. Holding out my hat to receive money, I tell her, "I'm collecting donations to help pay hospital expenses for my older brother. He needs — he gave a — kidney — to his best friend, and the insurance has run out." It sounds okay, considering I have no idea whether hospitals make live kidney donors pay, or if insurance policies cover that kind of thing.

Evidently she doesn't know, either. She picks up a little brown purse and takes out a five dollar bill. "I hope he has a speedy recovery."

"Thank you," I say, and mean it. Then I crumble under guilt and blurt out, "I'm sorry, that's all a fib, but we don't have money for breakfast and if you want it back, I'll understand."

She stares at me, startled and uncertain. Then she laughs. "Well, I get paid tomorrow, so take it. You look like you could use a hearty breakfast. And a pair of shoes."

My little toe sticks out of the right sneaker, my great toe out of the left. That landing in the gravel pit. "You're on the money there." I grin and salute her.

"Don't go next door," she cautions me. "Hit the computer people farther along."

"Thanks!" I take her advice and after telling the computer people mostly the truth, I have another five. Should I keep going while I'm on a roll, or take a break and feed Ernie before he faints?

From the relieved look on his face when he sees me, I'm glad I cut my begging short. "The lady in the computer store said there's a coffee shop just across from the old court house. Best pastries in town, and a latte to die for."

"Not sure I want to be near a court house."

"It's a museum now. The real one's across town."

"What are we waiting for?"

We're in a booth, eating a sensible breakfast of eggs and whole wheat toast, when two men in suits enter and sit right behind me. I don't pay much attention until the near one says, "How'd you do at East Wind?"

I choke and miss part of the other man's answer, but it ends "— escape with my life."

"And not much else, I bet," says the near man.

"Nobody's talking. If word gets out, they lose their funding."

"And you lose your reputation."

"Yours isn't too secure. Find Burand yet?"

The last is a dig, from his tone. I wonder who Burand is. But I wonder more who the speaker is, who's been nosing around East Wind. Looking for me?

"Vin — "

I make hushing motions, and Ernie blinks. He's ready to pay the bill, and I don't know whether to stay and try to hear more, or run out the back exit as fast as I can. One of those men probably knows my name, and might be carrying my photo.

The far guy says, "If he doesn't turn up by Monday, I'm going to write that story just the way I told you."

"And get yourself shot out of the saddle."

Since what I've heard doesn't make sense, especially the part about losing their funding, I listen harder.

"Poor bastard's probably on a fishing trip, doesn't even know his wife's been murdered."

"Why do you care?"

"His brother hired me to find him. To break the news gently."

"If he doesn't break your skull with an ax handle. That's what he used, wasn't it?"

He can't be talking about me. They're after Burand, my ghostly Actor, better known as John, who bashed his wife with an ax and threw her down the abandoned well. That's why he was asking questions at East Wind.

I motion Ernie to pay the bill, and drink the last of my latte. It's delicious.

To be on the safe side, I steer my adopted older brother out the back door of the coffee house and into the alley. Across a parking lot and into a green shady park. Leaves overhead rustle in a sweet breeze. We eat the pastries there, with a regular coffee to-go, and life is fine. I'm still puzzled about the funding, but figure it doesn't matter.

Ernie sits up from a snooze on the grass and stops mid-stretch. "Oh-my-God."

"What?" I'm lying on my back, dreaming of watermelon. Make a mental note to find a farmers' market before our money runs out.

"There's that pink Caddy."

Episode 9

Ernie's halfway down a long grassy slope, galloping like he's chasing a runaway dog or something. Low-hanging branches block some of my view of the street beyond, but I can see drivers on the tarmac and businesses across it. I don't see any pink car, and I figure he'll be back in a few minutes, but he isn't.

Well, I have the bedroll with his change of clothes and Hoodoo's gun strapped inside. But he has any leftover money, so I pick up my duffel and off I go to find him. If he catches up to the Caddy (doubtful), I wonder whether he'll just gaze at it from afar, wheedle his way into a ride, or steal the damn thing. Make that 'try to.'

I'm betting on the wheedling, so when I leap off the rock wall bordering the park and spot John gassing up at a small filling station, I'm not surprised that Ernie's jawing with him like they're old friends.

The traffic light changes and I saunter over to where they're opening doors and popping the hood and John's bragging on the finer points. I want a better look at him, since the glimpses I've had so far have left me without a clue what kind of guy he really is. He still looks like an actor, dressed now in jeans and penny loafers, and a pink shirt that's vaguely country style. Sunglasses hide his eyes. That sends a shiver over me. "Shades of Al."

I don't realize I've said it out loud until John turns to me. Ernie's busy stroking the leather seats. I'm not big on cars, like most of my dorm mates, but if I did own one with the power to turn Ernie into a marshmallow, I'd probably tell him to wash his hands before touching it. John looks like he might want to do that, too, and I wonder what's stopping him.

Ernie finally notices me. "Did you ever see anything so sweet?"

"No," I answer honestly. Pastel pink with a black top and lower panels, dark gray interior. Not my style, but show room clean. Expensive when somebody drove it home, and more expensive fifty years later.

Its owner holds out his hand. I'm floored when he says, "I'm John Collier. You fellows want to take a ride in her?"

His voice is the one I heard only a couple of nights ago when Ernie and I holed up in the shed, I'd swear to it. How coincidental could it be that the Suits in the coffee shop are looking for a John Burand? Are they the one and same, and is this smiling man shaking my hand a murderer?

Ernie's eyes light up at the offer. Then he shakes his head. "Dad would ground us forever if he found out we got into a car with someone we don't know."

"You won't tell, will you?" John asks me, and I choke up. I wish I had somebody to tell. The friendly smile leaves, but his voice is calm. "Think about it. Not every day you see a lady like this one."

John goes inside to pay for the gas, and when Ernie doesn't move, I pluck at his shirt sleeve. "Come on, bro." I haven't told him about Al, so he can't understand the panic I'm feeling.

"He's right. We'll never see another, much less ride in it."

"What's with you and this car? Sure, it's neat, but I think he's lying about his name. Ernie, I saw them bring a body up out of a well near Hackett last week. She was blonde, and you heard that man talking to John about the cops thinking he did it. Don't you recognize his voice?"

John's coming back. He'll get in the Caddy and drive away. That's what Ernie's dreading, I can tell by his glance toward me, eyebrows questioning, wanting me to agree to climb into the car and take a joy ride with a man who might have bashed his wife's head in with an ax handle.

"Just around the block," Ernie wheedles, but I'm not falling for it. Once inside and moving, we're hostages. Kidnapped and tortured. Never heard from again. I see my face on a Missing Child poster.

"Omigosh." I DO see a face on a Missing Child poster. Francine's copied photo, pinned in the middle of a flyer kiosk next to the newspaper boxes and propane gas bottle bin. Ernie's eyes follow and he goes pale and starts to shake. He walks over to the picture and studies it like he's planning on collecting a reward.

"What?" John sees nothing that scares him. He opens the driver's door, pauses to give us one last chance.

I have a clear view of the coffee shop two blocks up the hill. The Suits come out and stand on the sidewalk. My heart starts thumping hard. One of them is after John Burand, the other could be after me. If they spot the car, we're toast. "Mister Collier," I say, making conversation, "do you have a brother?"

"No," he answers, "why do you ask?"

One of the Suits lights a cigarette. The other heads down the hill toward his parked car. They'll be on the move any minute, maybe coming this way.

"Call me John. Make up your minds. I'm on vacation and don't want to waste another minute of it."

The second Suit halts in his tracks, then calls out and motions to his buddy, and I can't risk staying if he's seen me. "Ernie! Let's go!" I toss our gear into the back seat, tumble in after it, and close the door. Ernie doesn't hesitate. He and John give each other a grin and we're off. I keep looking for a pursuer until we turn a corner, but we're not pursued.

John pulls the Caddy smoothly onto an Interstate, headed east. I'm thinking about the Missing Child poster, when a sign stuns me. Dentonville, 50 miles.

"John, you got a road map?"

"Afraid not. I know where I'm going."

He has the advantage. Don't know where I'm going, or where I've been. "Where are you going? I thought it was 'just around the block.'" Out of the frying pan, into the fire, I think, already regretting what might be the most dangerous thing I've done so far.

"Can't feel her wings going twenty miles an hour and stopping every few feet for a light."

The speedometer creeps past fifty, sixty, hovers around seventy. The straightaway reaches to the horizon, and there's light traffic. When he does have to pass another car, the smooth moves of driver and car impress even me. I'm relieved when a speed limit sign whizzes by. 70 is okay here. He's careful not to exceed it.

"Just had her at a car show in Taylor," he's telling Ernie. "Took first place." He nods toward the glove compartment, and Ernie takes out a gaudy blue ribbon. There's no date on it. Why do I suspect he's lying? Maybe he is who he says he is. The Suits didn't seem to get exercised over seeing the car. If they did see it. Maybe all the guy wanted was to bum a cigarette off his pal.

I relax. A little bit. After all, Dentonville is where I was supposed to go.

But we turn off long before we make that 50 miles. It's a rest area, for which I'm thankful since the latte was a large one. We all go inside, and when I come out they've gotten into the Caddy, parked as usual in the most sheltered spot away from other vehicles. It dawns on me that he's not hiding it, but protecting the paint from dings and the doors from dents.

I'm filling up at the water fountain when I notice a blue SUV at the other end of the roadway. Fran jumps out, slams the door, and Hoodoo hangs out his window and yells, "You're crazy, you know that?"

She yells back, "Somebody might have turned it in. There are good people in the world, asshole."

Whatever she's lost, it's important to her. I hope it isn't Ernie's credit card. Then I remember: he canceled it. Running to the Caddy, I argue with myself about whether to tell him they're here. He's not going to win any fights with Hoodoo, and I doubt Fran would climb into the car with us even if she and her sweetie do talk trash to each other.

John checks the rear-view for traffic, mutters, "Crap." Ducks down, jostling Ernie against the door. "Drive." Ernie says "What?" John answers, "You want to drive or not?"

The second Ernie's out of the way, John's in the passenger seat, crouched out of sight. I watch Ernie walk around the rear of the car, and my breath stops. One of the Suits cruises by, craning his neck, and he's not looking for a parking space.

All my fears flood over me. I can't be sure he's not after me. He could be the one paid by John's brother—the one he claims not to have. Why doesn't he want to be found, unless his name really is Burand and he's wanted for murder?

Giving me a shrug, not caring why his dream is coming true, Ernie slides into the driver's seat. He backs into the roadway, smiling. Makes it halfway to the exit when he brakes, throwing me forward into John's seat.

"What the hell?" John's annoyed. But he stays below the windows.

Ernie's gaze is locked on Francine, getting into the SUV. I can feel the whirling of his brain, considering and rejecting courses of action. John's cold voice says, "Drive, damn you."

Ernie glances down, and I see John's hand pressing a gun barrel into his ribs. It must have been under the seat, within easy reach. Trembling, I feel inside the blanket bed roll and find Hoodoo's pistol. My arm has a life of its own. My weapon nudges John's shoulder and I tell him, "Two can play this game."

"Put it away, Vinnie." Ernie accelerates slightly and we pass the SUV without being noticed. We pass the Suit's car but it's empty. The Interstate is just ahead, and once we're rocketing into the unknown there'll be no turning back.

I poke John's shoulder gently. "Blink."

He laughs. Sits up. Smiling, he tucks his gun in the glove compartment. "Gutsy little devil, aren't you?"

Ernie lets out a sigh. He's committed now, but checks the rear view from time to time. There's no blue SUV in sight.

"Where are we going?"

"Thought we might pitch a tent, do some fishing."

Either he's crazy, or I am. Tent? Fishing? He acts like we've been friends and neighbors for years, that nobody will be looking for us or be concerned when we don't show up at home tonight. That much is true, but how can he be sure?

"The Suit didn't recognize the car," I say, puzzled. "But he would know you."

"Yeah, nobody can connect me to this baby. She's been laying low."

"In case of an emergency."

"You might say that."

I put Hoodoo's gun in its blanket nest. My hand's still shaking.

We pass a sign that says 'Dentonville - 30 miles.' What would I be doing, if I'd managed to go there? Never tried to help Al, or made friends with a crew of 'hipsies.' Could I have lied my way into a job, forged parental signatures on work papers? Signed into a motel, or convinced some lady to give me a room in her boarding house? I'll never know.

Wherever that road would have led, it had to be less interesting than what I'm doing now.

Half an hour passes. Scenery remains pretty much the same, concrete stretching to an ever-changing horizon, with glimpses of houses or car lots or restaurant strips dotting the picture. We must be near Dentonville when John speaks.

"Take the next exit."

Ernie obeys. There's a campground sign announcing 'Cozy Bear - 10 miles' but we turn in the opposite direction. "I know a back door to the place," John explains, reading my mind.

We're out in the sticks, off a two-lane and into the forest. The road's paved though barely wide enough for two cars to pass each other. Ernie's tense, not enjoying the ride as much as he'd thought he would. He's finally convinced that everything John's claimed to be is a lie. Didn't take a gun in my ribs, but then I'm fast learning that you can't trust anyone.

Well. Almost anyone. Ernie's on my trust list, for now anyway.

The asphalt ends and we're winding along a narrow dirt road. John flinches as underbrush rakes the sides of the car, but Ernie's doing his best and they're both silent.

We come to a gate. John takes a key from his shirt pocket and gives it to me. I push through the brambles to unlock it. Once the

Caddy's through, I secure the gate behind us. The click sounds like the cocking of an old West gun.

John motions me to return the key. Deeper into the forest. So deep I can't help asking, "Where's the campground?"

"Around the next curve. Nice little clearing, not far from the best trout stream you'll ever meet."

Little clearing is right. Only big enough for the tent John hauls out of the trunk, and a fire ring that's already there. A shaft of sunlight slants down, coming from the west. Low enough to be supper time, with night not far behind. There's fishing gear, too, like he said. Fly rods, bamboo rods, tackle. A cooler. A cardboard box. An old suitcase.

I reach for the suitcase. John waves me aside and closes the trunk lid. "Help your brother set up the tent. Get a fire going. There's burgers and drinks in the cooler. Buns and stuff in the box. I'll check out the stream."

John disappears into the dappled woods. There's maybe a faint trace of path, the kind you could lose your way on in a hurry.

"Come on, Vinnie, help me figure this mess out."

"I thought you were good at a lot of things." My taunt is joking and Ernie takes it that way. We lay out the stakes and poles and ropes, and finally have the tent standing. It's crisp and new and hard to handle. The fishing stuff looks just-bought, too, so I know this trip isn't to catch trout or bass or whatever's in the stream. If there is a stream.

John's taken the key with him, so we can't drive the car away. I'm curious about that suitcase he didn't want me touching. "Okay, bro, time to put your real skills to work."

Ernie's lifting a six-pack out of the cooler. "Want a drink?"

"I don't want to get drunk again. Bring your knife and let's see what's in the suitcase."

He hunkers at the trunk. Works at the latch. I watch the leafy shadows, hoping John won't catch us. "Weren't you scared when he pointed that gun at you?"

"Hoodoo pointing a gun at me would be scary."

"What's the difference?"

"Hoodoo's crazy enough to pull the trigger."

"And John isn't?"

"He's under pressure, but he's clear-headed. It's to his advantage not to kill the prisoners."

I hear the unspoken ending to that thought: until he has to.

"Wish I had Fran's nail file."

There's nothing in my duffel that's sharper than the pocket knife's smaller blade. I check the glove compartment but come up empty. I feel under the seat. John's gun is gone.

"He took it with him," I tell Ernie. "Gonna shoot somebody, I bet."

"We'll hear him if he does. There's no silencer on that gun."

Ah! That explains Ernie's cool. He knew John wouldn't fire in a public place. But we're not in a public place now.

The trunk lid slowly rises. "Watch for him."

"You watch. I want to open it." I haul the suitcase toward me and snap the old-fashioned fasteners. Neatly-folded clothing. A plastic bag for shaving stuff.

And a brown paper grocery bag, the top rolled tightly down a couple of inches. I pick it up. Not too heavy, not light, packed full of something that gives when I squeeze. Peeking inside, I can't believe my eyes.

Episode 10

"It is him! Here's Jordan's money." Stacks of bills, twenties, fifties, and hundreds, with little paper bands holding them.

Ernie's not watching the leafy shadows to make sure John doesn't catch us pawing through his suitcase. He's gathered sticks for a campfire, like he really thinks this is what we're doing here. Lays a thawed burger on the grate. "You want one or two?"

"Gimme two. I already got the million dollars I wished for."

He adds twigs to his fire and comes to look in the grocery bag. "Nah. Half, maybe."

I roll the top tight, the way it was, and stow the loot with the clothes and ditty bag. Slide the suitcase to its spot in the trunk. Lower the lid and am relieved when the catch works. "Good thing you didn't break the latch. He'd shoot you for sure, if you messed up his sweetheart."

I meant the Caddy, but I'm reminded: somebody he called Jordan did mess up his sweetheart. Loaded for bear — not the 'cozy' campground kind — John must believe he's close by.

Ernie lays more burgers on the grate. "So does the money convince you there is a guy named Jordan and John's not the villain?"

I'm not sure what to think. There's a gory story here, and I'd feel better if we heard it from John's mouth. "He might — " Pistol shots. Three of them, pop pop pop.

Not far away. Our eyes meet over the smoky fire. Can't say either of us is surprised, more like I-told-you-so fear.

A rifle answers, just like on tv. Now we're startled. Did he know someone was out there, and where to find him? Or was it accidental, coincidental? More pistol shots, so John's still in the game.

We wait, twitching with nerves. I want to go see what's happening but have better sense than to show myself where people are shooting at each other. Ernie flips the burgers with a butcher knife he's found in John's gear. He lays buns on the cooler lid, takes a drink from his beer can.

"You're awful calm." I resist the urge to bounce from foot to foot, or set out running toward the paved road we came in on. "Can't bullets travel, like from there to here? I'm not ready to die."

"What do you suggest we do? Hide in the car? Whoever's shooting that rifle would like nothing better than filling it full of holes. Except maybe to off John."

Grabbing Ernie's arm, I pull him down beside me in the dust behind the Caddy. "At least quit skylining yourself."

"Damn, you made me spill half the beer." He rolls onto his back. Still calm, even thoughtful.

"Give me a swig. I need it." Not easy, without a straw.

The can's frosty from the ice in the cooler, and the cold liquid splashes my chin. We listen, but no more shots are fired from either weapon. The burgers are burning.

Ernie crawls to them like a commando and a laugh escapes me. He glances over his shoulder and grins. "You got a death wish, bro," I say, joking. Then my gut tells me there's too much truth in the words for it to be funny. 'Some missions fail' he'd said, and the humiliation of going home a failure is as unthinkable to him as it is to me. I wonder who he's unwilling to face. Rather die, than face.

"Smells like supper's ready."

I peer underneath the Caddy and see John's feet in their penny loafers coming back from the fight. As I sit up, my hand clenches the empty beer can, crushing it. Hunkered next to the fire, Ernie uses the butcher knife to pick charred burgers off the grate and lay them on the open buns.

"Fish biting?" he asks.

John leans against his car. "Yeah. Didn't catch anything, though."

My mouth opens but what was trying to come out is stupid. Can't catch fish if you forget the bait. My two companions seem to be on the same wave length, while ol' Mouse lags a couple of beats behind, as usual.

John takes a can from the cooler and gulps a long swallow, as if he thinks we didn't hear anything unusual, like guns in the woods. If Ernie's dying to ask for details, he doesn't show it. I am, and I do, even if the vibes coming off me are invisible. John cuts his glance at me. "After we eat, I want to show you guys something."

All I want to see is us on the road out of here. I wonder if he'll show us the bag of money, and whether I can fake enough surprise so he doesn't catch on that it's no surprise. Or will he guide us through the woods to a dead body and make us bury it? Seen enough dead bodies to last me awhile, like forever.

I help myself to another frosty can. There's only one left. I toss it to Ernie, since it was my fault most of his got spilled. In the burger-chewing silence, I figure out this much: John hasn't killed anybody. . . Yet.

"Leaving her here?" Ernie gathers up the empties, stuffs them into the cardboard rack. Cleans the butcher knife in the sand.

"Not on your life."

We're leaving the tent. Ernie scatters the embers and heaps dirt on them. Two beers must have tipped my wicket, since I hear myself saying, "How're you going to get this big car through that little path?"

John grinds a half-smoked cigarette under his heel and grins. "Magic."

They get in. My mouth keeps talking. "If I follow the trail, will I end up where you're going?"

John swivels his head to look at me, a mixture of amusement and irritation on his face. "Try it and see." He nudges Ernie to close the back door and guides the car down the narrow passage.

The motor runs so smooth I can't hear it past the first bend. Did John stop to wait for me to come to my senses and catch up to them? Or is he still threading the Caddy toward a turnoff I didn't notice on the way in, which will land him where this track ends?

Curiosity overrides any doubt. I want to know where he went, where the shooting took place, and guess he's going there now. I'm jogging through forest with little undergrowth, damp pine needles and leaf mold underfoot, a light summer sky above, the rush of a small river off to my left. Pause to take a pee. A few birds flit among branches, and it's a peaceful moment. I plan to remember it for the rest of my life.

The path's shorter than I expect. At the wood's edge, wary as an animal sniffing for danger in the open space ahead, I'm stunned to find a place I know.

A one-story farmhouse, sitting forlorn in a ragged yard surrounded by fallow fields. An unpainted garage. The same shed where Ernie and I took refuge our first night together, and heard John and his mysterious friend exchange words, blows, and a grocery sack of money.

We've been going in circles.

And I still have no idea where I am. Hunkering behind a bush I can see through, I wait. What if they don't come back? My duffel bag is in the Caddy. Everything's in the Caddy.

No traffic on this road. Ernie and I walked for miles along it, evening and morning, and not a single car passed the whole time. There's a screened-in back porch on the run-down farm house. The outside spigot where I drank the rusty water. A closed door at the back of the garage, and I hope the front bay is open, in case I have to sleep there again.

Something moves.

About a quarter mile away, where woods and field meet, the bold nose of the Caddy inches forward. Stops. He waits, too, watching before showing himself. "What an optimist," I say aloud. If I can spot him, so can anyone lying concealed with a rifle. My mouth goes dry and my heartbeat quickens. Curtains covering the windows I can see, don't move. Evidently the ones on the other side give no alarm either.

The car emerges and quickly crosses the field. Grateful that I'm not alone and will probably sleep in a house tonight, I race to meet them.

John pulls close behind the shed. Ernie gets out and unlocks the overhead door, which creaks up slowly. All safe inside, he rescues our bed roll and duffel. John unfolds a custom cover — not the tarp we used the other night — and they place it over the car.

"You don't think he'll come back tonight?"

"He's tied up with paperwork in the hospital emergency."

Skid marks in the gravel show he left in a hurry. We climb three wooden steps to the screened porch. The lock's been broken. I bite my tongue to keep quiet about Ernie's lock-picking

80

skills. Best if John doesn't know. He leads us through a kitchen and down a short hall to a living room. "No lights," he cautions. "Ever."

There's enough daylight that I can see this place hasn't been updated for forty years. Like the last foster home I stayed in, except there are no crying babies or toys scattered everywhere.

Fresh spots stagger across the brown and gold shag rug, a blood trail through the house. Glass litters the carpet beneath a broken front window. Inexpensive brown and gold sofa and two matching chairs, a few side tables with lamps, a console tv, and a wall phone.

Bedrooms on either side, a bathroom next to what's probably a door to the cellar. Whoever built this place never gave a thought to how dangerous it is to put a bathroom next to cellar steps. That's how Jerry's grandmother met her end. A tumble headfirst in the night, when she expected a solid floor under her reaching foot. At least, that's what he told us.

"Why didn't she have a night light?" Steve had asked. "Why didn't she count the doors? She must have gone to the potty a zillion times. She should have known which was which."

It's the only time I ever saw Jerry's eyes fill with tears. "You don't know what you're talking about, so just shut up."

Months later we decided his grandmother had been too sick to remember to switch on the night light before she went to bed. Or medication had clouded her mind. Or maybe the house where she died wasn't the one she'd been used to. I never told Jerry I finally understood. If the phone works, maybe I'll do that tonight.

Those glass shards will be the devil to vacuum up. Slouched in one of the easy chairs, I hear long-ago voices. His is soft, hers isn't. What was her name? She used to wear a loose 'house dress' and bedroom slippers all day. I was the oldest, eight or close to nine. It's where I learned about carpets and windows. She hated those jobs. So did I. Heavy vacuum cleaner, lots of broken glass. When he lost his job, I was sent back to East Wind. This is the first real house I've been inside since then.

John brings a large photo album from a cabinet under some built-in bookshelves (empty), and motions Ernie to the sofa beside him. Got to be the car. Ernie asks questions, makes appreciative noises. John's wound up, giving the history. I start to realize the Caddy's more special than I'd thought.

"Even with employee discount, he had to mortgage the house to make payments. Mother nearly left him over it, more than once. When she got that dinky watch as severance for twenty-five years of service in the textile mill, she wanted him to sell the car, but he had only a few installments left. He took a second job as a security guard. Kept her scared all the time."

"What did she cost new, John?" I ask, meaning the car. He looks around as if he's forgotten I'm there, or is surprised that I'm finally showing some interest.

"With the trimmings, tax, and shipping, close to fourteen thousand dollars."

It doesn't sound like much. Collins keeps telling me if my grades stay high, I'll write my own ticket to college, end up earning ninety thousand a year. He never says at what, but I have to hope he's right.

Ernie stares into space, thoughtful. I can tell it sounds like peanuts to him, too.

"Dad had a passion for that Caddy from the day he first laid eyes on her. Said she was a better investment than money in the bank. And he was right."

"What's she worth now?" I join them for a look at the photos, thinking again about the stacks of money locked in her trunk.

Ernie comes out of his trance. "Vinnie, this car's a legend on the Internet. Rare even in restored condition, and John's is as near mint as it can be."

"So that's what you and Jordan are fighting about?" Again the wrong thing.

John slaps the album shut. "No. I told you, nobody alive can connect me to the car. It's my only chance to stay a ghost long enough to do what I'm going to do."

Remembering that wild ghostly wailing that spooked me the other night, I shiver. Now the ghost is sitting here in his old home, calm with rage.

"He charmed Margie but he'll never get anything else away from me." John replaces the album in the cabinet. "I'm not through with him."

Mouse clamps down on the need to blurt out about seeing Margie dragged up from a well naked except for one red shoe, but can't help asking. "Why would he kill her?"

"Because she married me."

It goes unsaid that Jordan broke into John's—or his parents' house—to search for his getaway cash, which John's nameless ex-friend had stolen and gave to him in the middle of a night not a week ago. Nice move, John.

Ernie's voice is reasonable. "You need to tell your side. Let the authorities deal with Jordan."

"And pay some sleaze lawyer to lose the case? I'd have to sell the car, and I'll never do that. She's all I have left."

Mouse clamps down again to keep from mentioning the loot in the grocery bag. I know John hasn't forgotten it for a second. So he's still lying about that. Keeping it secret, anyway. Would he have an explanation if I told him we'd found it? Or would he whip out that pistol and shoot us dead?

I want to trust him. I like him, in fact. Riding in the Caddy is more fun than walking, and wondering where this adventure will take me next keeps me on an exciting edge. Dusk is fast closing in, storm clouds gathering. "Who's on first watch?"

They look at each other. "I will," Ernie volunteers. "The kid needs his beauty sleep and you probably could use a snooze."

John hands him the pistol. "Wake me before you need to use it, if you can." He goes into the front bedroom and closes the door.

Ernie makes sure the safety's on, and lays the gun on a table.

I pick up the phone to see if it works, and it does. I could call East Wind. "What did he tell you?"

"Not much. After Margie left him, he sold their home and came here to lick his wounds. That's why the power's still on. She'd been gone almost a year when she called him one night and said she was afraid of Jordan." Ernie wipes his forehead with the tail of his shirt. "Called again two weeks ago. Wanted him to meet her, take her back. He hung up on her."

No wonder John's a mess. Filled with guilt. Suddenly his wailing makes sense. It's not only grief over her death, it's guilt that his action could have caused it. There's nothing I can do to help him. Or Ernie, torn up over Francine and stuff that's not his fault. We both start for the wall phone.

"You first," I say, partly to hear who he's ready to spill to, mostly because I'm not. Any contact with East Wind might send me in a direction I don't want to go. He lifts the phone, dials a long-distance number, hunkers with his back to me. It rings awhile before he says into the mouthpiece, "Dad?"

While I'm antsy to stay and eavesdrop, his body tells me he wants privacy. I go into the other bedroom.

Twin beds, a single window overlooking the back yard. Two dressers, cheap pictures on the walls, framed 8 x 10 studio portraits of a middle-aged couple on both dressers. It's too dimly lit to gather much from their faces. Was this always the parents' room, or did John and his maybe-brother share growing-up secrets? There's no evidence left of a childhood, if they did.

An ancient central air unit kicks on. The broken front window will make it run most of the night, just noisy enough to let a lurker sneak up on us and climb through it. I try to raise the window in here, but it's painted shut. At least no one will get in that way.

An old radio sits next to a lamp on the stand between the beds. So it doesn't blare its message to the rest of the house, I turn the volume knob to the left before clicking it on, then adjust so it's talking only to me.

Tuned to a station playing soft music. I stretch out on one of the beds and close my eyes. Seems a lifetime since Ernie and I broke into the Haw Creek Elementary School, longer since those other nights on the road. This must be number five. By far the most comfortable. My mind starts to relax. Then two things happen.

The first is an idea that comes as I'm drifting over the edge of sleep. John said, 'No one alive knows about the Caddy.' But Margie must have. What if she told Jordan?

I'm off the bed, intending to wake him with this when there's a news break. A man's radio voice says ". . . reporting on the twelve-year-old missing from East Wind."

Episode 11

Don't dare turn up the volume, so I lay my head next to the radio as it spreads the news.

". . . No new developments in the disappearance last Saturday night of a student from the East Wind School for Boys. Authorities are not ruling out the possibility of a kidnapping, although no demands for a ransom have — "

So my buddies haven't pinned the blame on me, and if I know Steve and Jerry, they'll deny everything till doom's day. The Suit in the coffee shop, the one I call Reporter, didn't learn their secrets. How did he even know to ask?

The newsbit ends with ". . . an anonymous tip." I bet Collins freaked when he did bed check and found me gone. He'd never come forward, with either his name or mine. O'Leary would fire his ass so quick he wouldn't have time to pack. Bad enough that the news got leaked. But who leaked it?

I go into the dark living room to tell Ernie, but he isn't there. Faint moonlight slants through the kitchen window and panes in the top of the door. He's at the table, which he's dragged to block that entrance, since Jordan broke the lock to get in. He doesn't hear my bare footsteps on the linoleum, but he's not asleep on his watch.

There's a short-wave radio in front of him. He feels my presence before I join him. Turning, he whispers, "Listen to this." I sit down and he puts the earphones on me.

". . . at large. The suspect is armed and believed to be dangerous. Anyone answering his description should be reported to local law enforcement officers immediately."

I don't have to ask whose description. He is armed, but dangerous only to Jordan. And himself. His gun's on the table beside the short-wave. "You know how to use that thing?"

Ernie says, "Yeah." I wait for more, but he takes back the headset and turns off the radio. "I'm on the news, too," I tell him, "but they don't have a clue."

"Lucky."

That's his total reaction to my fifteen seconds of fame. Is he thinking instead of Francine's face on the "missing child" poster we saw in town? Talk about being in the public eye. Guess I shouldn't ask what he and his dad said to each other on the phone earlier.

We listen to the silence of a summer night on a lonely road. A few hot weather insects are gearing up for their concert. The ancient central air unit has shut off. Maybe for good.

Would we hear Jordan sneaking up on us? I wonder how badly he's wounded. Glass still litters the shag carpet under the broken living room window, and I file a mental note not to walk there barefoot.

"I thought you were going to sleep." Ernie's prowling, peering out windows. Either he watches too many movies or too much tv, or he's a natural at this.

"I thought so, too. What time is it?"

"Nowhere near time to wake John. If he's sleeping."

"If I'd just sent somebody to an emergency room, I'd be having nightmares." Sending an enemy to the hospital, I figure, is the least of John's nightmares. "Didn't he tell you anything else about Margie?" I can still see her blue-blotched body and red shoe, but only when I'm awake.

"He never said as much, but he loved her. She didn't love him. Not enough, anyway. They'd had a few problems, mostly over money. She met Jordan in a safe singles club, cried on his shoulder. He made her think she wanted a divorce."

"John's divorced?"

"No. That's what they couldn't stand. He wouldn't let her go."

Considering that, if it's all true, I can see how John might be the one to kill her. Chills dart along my spine as I realize what I've just thought.

"Go back to bed, Vinnie. I'm in charge. For a change." He holds up the gun in his hand, and plants himself in one of the easy chairs. Its vantage point covers both porches.

Doubtful about access to the bedrooms, not to mention the bathroom and — worse — the basement, I check the former for myself. The high window is too small for even my butt to wiggle through, and I sense a drop off on this side of the house. Jordan would need to be rail-thin and have a ladder to get in that way.

"Ernie. This cellar door doesn't have a lock."

"The outside one does. And the steps creak."

Satisfied, I say good night and am asleep moments after my head hits the pillow.

They don't wake me for my turn at watching. Is it because they think a kid like me can't do the job? It's not light yet, but will be in half an hour. Ernie's dead to the world on the other twin bed. Through the open door I can hear shower water hitting the old-fashioned enameled tub. I put on my sneakers and go into the kitchen.

In the fridge I find a carton with six eggs, half a loaf of bread, and an opened package of bacon. Yum! There's also a couple of six-packs and a wilty head of lettuce. A bar of cheddar cheese. Several closed containers that remind me of Francine.

I wonder where she and Hoodoo are now, and whether he's discovered his gun is missing. Bet he can't imagine Ernie sneaking into the SUV and stealing it.

Rummaging in the freezer I find a package of coffee and on the counter there's a coffee maker with a glass pot. I've never made coffee before, only lately discovered how much I like it. Each of us will probably want a couple cups, so I measure six cups of water into the pot. So far so good. Now, what to do with it?

I'm back in that last foster home, and strain my brain to remember what she-of-the-forgotten-name used to do. But her pot was different. A tall chrome thing that had some kind of insides that I washed a million times. She made sure I understood I was NEVER to wash the pot in the sink because of the electric cord plug-in. There was a long stem on a flat stand, and a little basket that fit down over it.

"Basket . . . Basket." The coffee has to go somewhere. It's pretty clear where the water goes, so I do that. I examine the maker. This must be where it comes out, so I try to get into the part I think should come off. It doesn't budge. I lift and pull and push, until by accident there's a click and a different part swings to the side. It holds an old soggy paper like the ones cupcakes are baked in, only bigger. Full of grounds. I trash that and look for a clean one. Finally find a box labeled "filters" in an overhead cabinet.

"Doin' good," I tell myself. Fill the filter and swing the basket into place. Press the switch and it turns red. I hear the water begin to bubble. Turn to the stove, find a nonstick pan in the drawer beneath. Find butter in a compartment in the fridge door. Locate the bowls and plates and cups.

I could live like this forever. Then John emerges in clean clothes, shaved, his face slack with weariness, and I remember Jordan might get out of the hospital today, and the cops are heating up their search.

"You can cook?" He gives me a one-sided grin.

"Just getting it ready for you. I made coffee."

"Thank God," he says, and peels off slices of bacon.

He's sizzling up a pan of food that makes my mouth water when Ernie staggers through, on his way toward the bathroom. "Coffee, black and plenty of it."

"Me, too." John flips the food, reaches for a plate. Bread pops up in the toaster. He takes out the browned slices, puts in four more.

I fill cups that his mother must have bought. They're not the he-man mugs I picture him drinking from.

He sets stuff on the bare table. The short-wave's on the other counter. Bet there was a table cloth with checks or flowers, when he was growing up here. "John, you told me you don't have a brother." The question's in my tone, not the words. He hears it.

"I don't. I had a sister, but she was lots older and left home when I was starting high school."

Wanting to trust him once and for all, I pursue this line of thought. "Remember when we met at the gas station, and all of a sudden we decided to jump in your car?"

He cuts me a sharp glance. "Yeah."

"Well, it wasn't to please Ernie, exactly."

"What exactly was it?"

We sit down opposite each other. Ernie joins us, taking the chair at the end of the table. "We were in a coffee house and I overheard two guys talking. One of them said your brother paid him to find you."

Ernie adds, "He was the one cruising behind us in the rest area, wasn't he? You knew him."

"He's Jordan's cousin. Thinks he's a damned detective."

"That's not good," Ernie mumbles, chewing bread and eggs and bacon.

John takes a long swallow from his cup. Sets it down so hard he spills some coffee on the table. "Good God, what did you put in this?"

Hair on the back of my neck stiffens. "Why? What's the matter?"

Ernie cautiously sips. "Strong enough to float an iron wedge."

I look at mine. It's black, all right. What Ernie said he wanted.

"Tastes like that stuff the fancy places serve in a thimble," John sneers.

Ernie whirls up from the table, picks up the pot. Starts toward the sink. When he tips the spout toward the drain, John grabs his arm. "Don't waste it!"

Ernie's rigid stance conveys something but I don't know what. Then he says, "You can afford it now."

My jaw drops. Here I've been keeping my lip zipped about the money, and Ernie spits it out in a tone I've heard him use only for Hoodoo.

John lets go of his arm like it's burned him. Takes hold of the bright silvery chain and hauls Ernie's medallion from inside his shirt collar. "Last night I got to thinking. Want to know what I thought?"

Ernie's mouth stays shut. Mine flies open. "I do."

John smiles, but it isn't friendly. "I thought, this guy's got enough dough to buy whatever he wants. What's he doing on my tail? All I have is the car. Does he want it? He can turn me in, and the spoils of war can be his."

That necklace again. The way the floozy blonde and the greedy cab driver kept fawning over it, I know it's valuable.

The upscale shirt, running shoes. Ernie's embarrassment over Francine's slutty behavior. The SUV, the credit card, the lack of real work skills. Stuff I knew, but all it took for John to wise up was that necklace. It screams 'rich boy' and this galls John.

Looking around me, it isn't hard to figure. Everything's old, worn, falling apart, outdated. A mother who probably worked and worried herself to death, a dad who never let that stop him from owning the most expensive thing in his world. Damn the torpedoes.

"Just chill, both of you." I don't want to lose our wheels or meals, and I can understand the effects of poverty on John's early years. But if our trio splits up, I'll have to choose Ernie. Whether he's rich or even mega-rich, he's real. John's in no shape to see that, only the signs of something he's always envied.

He lets go of Ernie's necklace. Ernie fills the pot with hot tap water. "This should solve your problem."

"Only one of them," John answers, but with less resentment. He accepts a cup and seems to have forgotten Ernie's comment that turned attention from my lack of coffee-making skills onto darker ground, as he doesn't mention the money in the Caddy trunk.

We eat in silence. I'm wondering if he counts me as a problem. Or am I really a kidnapped kid, a necessary hostage? Then, like he reads my mind, he says, "I would have taken you both back into town the way I promised, if I hadn't seen Cuz looking for me."

"Good thing he doesn't know about the car." Ernie pushes his plate aside. "You ought to at least paint her, John. Black, maybe."

I'm about to remember something, but coffee explodes out of John's nose. Hot words explode out of his mouth. "Paint her! I'd as soon — "

Whatever the finish, he leaves it unsaid. My brain fills in: '. . . kill my own mother." Jerry says that whenever anyone makes a stupid suggestion to him.

Ernie persists. "Sooner or later, someone you know will see you before you see him."

"One little detail I have to take care of, and I'm out of the country."

With Jordan's money. Or maybe it isn't Jordan's. John's friend stole it from him, but where'd the cash come from? I'm gearing up to spring a few questions, now that he's calmer. If John leaves the country, how hard would it be to leave with him? Would Ernie go? Depends on what he and his dad said on the phone last night. They haven't found Fran, or his mood wouldn't be so crabby. I think about his mom. Don't recall a single word about her.

"That little detail could get you killed." Ernie's sounding like an old man again.

John finishes his coffee, scoots his chair away from the table, lights a cigarette. He never smokes in the Caddy. Ernie refills his own cup and mine. I hope there's a dishwasher, other than me.

"If you're thinking it's insurance money, it's not."

"I never said that."

"How'd you get in the trunk?"

Ernie shows John his pocket knife. "How'd you know?"

"When I went out this morning to bring in the suitcase, the bag was turned wrong."

"Vinnie, we gotta be more careful next time."

It's nice, the way he doesn't point at me as the chief culprit, but I don't believe the bag was turned wrong. John picked up on Ernie's foot-in-the-mouth comment about being able to afford a fresh pot of coffee.

"If it's not her insurance, where did the money come from?" Ernie reaches for a cigarette and John offers him the pack and matches.

Death wish, I think, the boy's got a death wish.

Surprisingly, John doesn't take offense, just fields the question. "Out of Jordan's credit union account." He sends a smoke ring into the air over the table.

Ernie tries, but blowing smoke rings is not one of his skills. They both laugh.

Their return to easy banter makes me relax so I leave them alone long enough to go pee. On my way, movement along the paved road catches my eye, but it's just a car. Heading to a factory job that pays by piecework, like the one John's mom stuck with for twenty-five years.

He's itchy to complete his mission and get out of Dodge. Ernie's words 'Some missions fail' ring in my ears again. Whatever John's mission is, it's bound to be dangerous. I picture him marching into Jordan's hospital room—or going to his house, if he's out by now—and finishing the job. If he does, we'll be accomplices, before and after the fact. D-hall will seem like a picnic next to juvie.

And what will Ernie's dad think, say, do? Bad enough to have a daughter like Fran burning up the roads with a maniac like Hoodoo. Worse, to have a son who's meant to be in college and ends up in prison.

Once we leave here, we're never coming back. It's a neglected farmhouse now, but in spite of the family being poor they did the best they could with it. Those framed photos in the bedroom show people who loved each other. John's ditty bag is open on the counter. He hasn't used his safety razor because it's not wet. I open the mirrored medicine cabinet over the sink and see an ancient shaving mug with a brush and razor beside it. A bit of foam. The crater of damp soap in the bottom.

A wave of sadness sweeps over me, and I shake it off. Didn't know his dad. Didn't know his mom. And half of what I know about John could be false.

I brush my teeth and say goodbye to the tiny green-tiled bathroom where I wish there was time to shower. Maybe cut my hair.

Through the busted front door pane I hear stealthy feet creak the boards on the wooden porch. I race down the hallway to the kitchen. "We've got company!"

Episode 12

John leaps up, turning over his chair, and dashes down the cellar steps. I dash too but Ernie jerks me to a halt. "We can bluff whoever it is."

He picks up the chair, then dumps scraps from John's plate and shoves it and his fork and cup into a cabinet under the sink.

93

With the cigarette dangling from his lips and his unshaved face, he looks tough.

Rap! Rap! Rap! like somebody's used to being noticed. Would Jordan knock? I don't think so. John hasn't said how bad he was hit, but he was able to drive away, and the blood spots on the carpet didn't look too serious. Even so, he's not likely to be out of the hospital this early. But he could send cops to investigate.

My heart's racing, mouth's too dry to form words. I step to the end of the hall, where I can see a man peering in. Not sure whether he spots me. Not sure which Suit he is, but it is a suit he's wearing, and not a police uniform. His features are fuzzy through the dusty screen, his voice is like his knocking. Loud and bossy. "Open up, Burand. We want to talk to you."

Ernie's knuckles poke me in the spine. "Go let him in."

If it's 'Cuz' I don't want to let him in. Even a wannabe detective might know we're lying. He'll already have a question about that window pushing at his teeth, and if Jordan called him after the shooting he won't miss the blood trail on the rug.

If it's the reporter who took pictures of poor dead Margie, he could be the same reporter who scooped my departure from East Wind, and if he's been carrying my photo, I don't want him seeing me. A storm of pounding. Whoever thought up the line 'He who hesitates is lost' wasn't kidding.

I realize he said 'we' only seconds before someone behind us calls out, "You're wasting your energy, Bob."

Ernie and I whirl around. The table, still unwiped of breakfast crumbs, no longer blocks that entrance, so there was nothing to keep the tall blond man from walking right in. I'm guessing this is Cuz. He unlatches the door for Bob, who's hot and bothered though it's barely daylight. "Damn, you guys deaf or something?"

"Hard of hearing," Ernie says, straight-faced. Speaking makes him cough. He doesn't dare let go of the cigarette because Cuz is bound to pounce on it to see if it's John's brand.

"You fellows all right?" Cuz asks us.

"Why wouldn't we be?" I'm all innocent-eyed.

"Here by yourselves?" Reporter is the ambulance-chaser at the well, minus his camera, but if he recognizes me he's keeping mum. He stands outside the front bedroom, thinks twice about sticking his nose inside. Listens. Heaves a relieved sigh when no one blows his head off.

"School's over. We can be here." Ernie wanders around, lifts up a chair cushion. "Hey, bro, what'd you do with the remote?"

Cuz is checking the bathroom. I hope he doesn't open the medicine cabinet and notice the damp shaving brush. Ernie hasn't shaved in days and I don't have to yet. To divert him from the cellar, I ask, "Want some coffee? Mom always makes us be nice to visitors even if they do show up without an invitation."

He gives me a skeptical glance. "I'd appreciate a cup, thank you."

Reporter pushes open the door to the bedroom Ernie and I used. "Cold water or tea would suit me better."

There's ice in the fridge freezer, for which I'm thankful. I hand him the glass, he looks me in the eyes. "What're you two doing in this house? How long have you been here? Did you break that window?"

Ernie's politely pouring coffee and acts as if he's not listening, much less holding up his share of the bluff. I have to rely on my Boy Scout face. "We're vacationing. Rent's cheap and the fishing's supposed to be awesome. Sorry about the window. We'll pay for it."

"Where's Burand? We need to talk to him about an important matter."

Should I tell him we don't know anybody named Burand? John said his name's Collier. If that's his middle name, Cuz might know it, and I'd be sunk. Again I hesitate, but Ernie finds the remote, flips on the tv. The room vibrates with bells ringing, cheers, shouts, and a tune I hope doesn't stick in my brain the rest of the day.

I shrug. Bob the Reporter snatches the remote from him and hits the mute. Ernie blows a perfect smoke ring into his face. Luck or not, I choke back a laugh, it's so Hoodoo. Only, Hoodoo wouldn't cough and ruin the effect.

Standing in the hallway, Cuz forces down coffee. He makes a face after each slurp. "Damn, this stuff's weak."

Ernie marches to the counter, grabs the pot and dashes what's left into the sink. "Can't please anybody. To hell with critics." Strides to Bob, reaches for the remote. Bob refuses to give it to him.

"You try, Martin. I'm shooting blanks."

Ah. Cuz is Martin. Is it Martin Jordan, or is it Martin and Jordan Something Else? Guess it doesn't matter. A crooked sweat-path marks Ernie's temple, though the house is actually cool, since the air conditioning unit has kicked on. Is he having a hard time playing the delinquent? Stymied because Bob held on to the clicker?

Or . . . Has he decided to turn John in? Ugly scenario: John's in jail, car's impounded, Ernie Rich Boy buys it at auction for half its going rate.

Then he yells, "Man! I hate game shows." He stalks off to the bathroom and we hear him flush. No more cig. That clue's gone. If only we could so easily flush the Inquisition. But Martin's not finished with us.

"How'd you guys get here? I didn't see any car. And if you're fishing, where's your tackle?" He boldly walks into the front bedroom.

My heart nearly stops. John brought in the suitcase, and it's probably there. What if he finds Jordan's money?

"Yeah," Bob echoes. "Where's your fishing gear?"

"We rode a bus." Ernie sounds pissed, not scared. "The guy who booked our vacation said we could rent tackle at some cafe a couple miles down the road. You tellin me we been had?"

"If you paid Burand any money, you been had."

"Who's this Burand you keep talking about? We made a deal with an old guy named Ervin."

Ernie's still on our side. But his bad boy act is wearing thin. Martin comes out of the bedroom as if he hasn't found anything, and my breath starts flowing again. Then he reaches for the cellar door knob. My knees almost buckle. Ernie takes a step as if to stop him, but can't risk blowing our cover by hovering.

We wait. Bob turns on the tv, channel surfs, muted.

Martin's gone so long Ernie leans into the doorway and calls, "Hey, mister, I don't think the owner would like you snooping around."

When there's no reply, he clatters down the steps. I wish for a gallon of spring water to unstick my tongue from the roof of my mouth. Two sets of feet return and Martin reappears, Ernie behind him. Ernie's eyebrow shrug shows me John's long gone.

"How about the shed?" Bob suggests.

"That old garage? It's worth a look."

"Oh, you don't want to mess in there," I warn him. "We were told it's supposed to stay locked." Even if John made it into the woods, the Caddy's still in the shed. They know it's John's house, they'll soon know that's his car.

We all troop across the yard to the garage. Locked, front and back, but Martin kicks and kicks the rear latch until he knocks it off and the door slowly rises. First Jordan and now Cuz. Locksmiths in these parts must make a nice living.

Ernie's intake of breath tells me he's as surprised as I am. The two men move forward into the dark little building and poke around in the clutter lining the walls. No tracks in the dirt floor. No tracks in the gravel driveway. More of John's magic.

Bob props his hands on his hips, and his sweeping glance stops on me. "Say you two are brothers?"

Ernie pulls his billfold from a pocket. "Want my ID?"

Since I don't have any, I feel like kicking him, but his confidence has returned and apparently he's convinced Bob. The reporter brushes imaginary dirt off his hands. Ready to leave. I'm finally able to moisten my lips and swallow.

Martin is less willing to give up. He's noticed the field, where tire tracks flattened the grass. "Who's been driving out there?"

"How should I know? I don't have a car."

I add helpfully, "We haven't heard any cars except yours."

97

"Loneliest road I ever saw," Bob comments. I expect him to go on 'Except the one to East Wind' but he just picks his teeth with a fingernail.

It's not a good sign they're traveling together now. Even if Bob hasn't recognized me, Martin might work out a few kinks. The only place I can recall being seen with John is that gas station, and if the Suits asked questions there, some piece of the puzzle that's been missing could kick in.

A bigger puzzle is, Where's John? An even bigger one, Where's the Caddy? I know the bag of money's with one of them, but whether we'll see either again is doubtful.

Martin's staring over the field, cogs and wheels turning, when his cell phone rings. "Where are— He what? Which hospital?"

We watch the Suits hurry to their car and speed away. "Are you thinking what I'm thinking?" I ask.

He shakes his head. "He wouldn't leave us."

It wasn't what I was thinking. The call was a shock so they didn't know about the shooting when they showed up here. They'll zoom off to see Jordan in the hospital and we won't have to worry about them for awhile. Ernie's trust in John has the opposite effect: now I'm worried we might be stuck here and have to walk out. Again.

He goes into the house, where he plunders dresser drawers in John's bedroom, laying out socks, underwear, knit shirts, and trousers. "Bring me a grocery bag."

I take him a paper bag from beneath the sink. Run hot water into the basin and pile it full with all the mucky dishes. Add dishwashing liquid, so maybe ants and roaches won't overrun the place. Double check to be sure the coffee pot's off. If the house burns down, won't be my fault.

Fill another bag with packages of foods that will keep, like crackers and a jar of peanut butter, cookies and some pop-top individual servings of fruit and pudding, spoons and a case knife. What else? I grab the package of coffee, in case we ever land in another place where there's a pot and electricity. Next time, I'll know how to make it.

Ernie comes out of the bathroom. He's loaded his bag with who-knows-what, besides the clothes. John's shaving kit. Our toothbrushes and toothpaste, I hope.

"Ready?"

What choice is there, but to follow him. I pick up my duffel and our bed roll, sorry there wasn't a pair of shoes in John's stuff that would fit me.

We go down across the front yard to the paved road, and turn right. It's a long way to that abandoned service station where we lost Fran, but asking why he didn't choose the shorter route to town seems a waste of breath, and I need it to keep up with him. We jog for maybe five minutes before he cuts up through the woods on our right and I realize he's headed for John's campsite.

"What makes you think he's hanging around?"

"He needs us. Remember? Hostages. Cover."

If there's another word in his brain, he doesn't share.

"And we need him— why?"

No answer. I save ten other questions for when we're at the camp. Branches and blackberry briers slap my face and rip at my clothes. My feet slide on dead pine needles and the landing re-bruises my knees. I'm about to complain that we're lost, when we arrive.

No Caddy, not even the tent. Only the burned-out fire ring where we cooked the burgers. "Okay, bro. I'm going back to the house."

"Not yet." Ernie checks the sandy ground like a pioneer scout in an old tv show. "This way."

He leads me down a trail fainter than the one I enjoyed yesterday, and in an almost opposite direction. We push aside limber bush branches and stumble over sticks and hummocks of moss. My hat and sunglasses are no protection, being in the duffel, and the holes in my sneakers grow. It's times like this I wish I was at East Wind, serving my sentence in D-hall.

We come to a smaller clearing and there sits the Caddy, John in the driver's seat. "Took you long enough." He stashes the bulging grocery bags in the back and tosses Ernie the keys.

Ernie puts the keys in his pocket. Leans against the car. "First, let's clear the air. I don't give a damn about your opinion of me. Doesn't bother me that you're not satisfied with having the money but feel you have to kill Jordan. What does concern me is, we're apparently along for the ride. I'm okay with life on the run, but it's time to cut the kid loose."

Episode 13

"Whoa!" I yell. "Don't I have a vote?" All glowing thoughts of D-hall fall into dust like a stuck vampire.

"Get in the car." John's tone isn't menacing. "We'll talk on the way."

Shooting Ernie a look that I hope lets him know I feel betrayed, I get in the car. John goes round to the passenger side. We wait. A minute passes. Birds twitter in the bushes. An eighteen-wheeler changes gears on the Interstate, maybe half a mile away.

"Ernie's wrong about you wanting to kill Jordan, isn't he?"

John looks over his arm resting on the back of the seat. "No."

Fear ripples up my spine.

"I want to kill him. And I wish I had, when I shot him. But that's no longer the plan."

"What is the plan, John?" Ernie slides behind the wheel but doesn't start the engine.

"You just point us north. I'll tell you where to turn off."

He threads the Caddy along what John says is a logging road until we come out on a two-lane that leads to an Interstate ramp. Glad to be off that jaw-jarring track and into new territory, I wonder what he's got in mind. If he's not interested anymore in getting even with Jordan, is he going to turn him in to the police? Does he have enough evidence to bring him to trial? Or, is he afraid he'll be arrested. Maybe even convicted. North means Canada, and I'm not dressed for cold.

We drive maybe forty-five minutes, past fields and trees and a cow pasture. None of us has said a word, and I guess John has forgotten his promise to talk on the way. Or he's thinking up a bunch of lies to tell us. Feels like lunch time already, though I know we had breakfast less than an hour ago. I sneak a cracker out of my bag, but can't get the lid off a new jar of peanut butter.

Time flies when you're having fun.

A sign announces 'Glen Alpine, Next Exit.' John motions, and Ernie makes the signal. We zoom up the ramp. John gestures to the right and we turn onto a winding two-lane bordered by forest.

"Used to go fishing here with my dad when I was a kid. It's not likely anybody will know me. They have a festival. Food, music, games, rides, crafts, produce. And if we stay long enough, fireworks."

Produce and fireworks appeal to me most. If I don't put some greenery in my gut soon, my teeth will fall out. "It can't be the Fourth of July."

"It can be, but it's not." Ernie glances at me through the rear view and his smile begs forgiveness. I look away. He was ready to 'cut me loose' just when things are getting exciting, and that could mean only one thing— setting me off at the first available police station. For my own good, yeah, I know. He's older-brothering me the way he can't do anymore for Francine. Are she and Hoodoo still lost, captured, or free?

Will I see my own picture on a Missing Child poster in Glen Alpine? All this circling—or spiraling—has left me confused. "How far are we from—" No. Can't say Hackett, the scene of the body-dump, if not the crime itself. Don't dare say East Wind, or John might agree that returning me is a good idea after all. "—Dentonville."

"Twenty minutes if you keep to the speed limit. Why?"

Since I no longer want to go there, and the information hasn't helped me anyway as I'm clueless about where any place is, relative to any other place, I answer, "Just curious."

"Nothing in Dentonville to be curious about. It's an almost-city with strips."

Ernie gives a snort. "That's Hoodoo's speed, all right."

For a moment I'm puzzled. I wouldn't have thought Hoodoo would spend a dime in a mall or shopping center. Then Ernie's meaning seeps through my skull. John doesn't ask who he's talking about, mainly because he's looking for another turn off.

This one's a twin to the Cozy Bear Campground entrance, and I think Uh-oh. He really does mean to camp and fish, with Suits crawling out of the woodwork. Once Jordan and his cousin Martin and Bob the Reporter finish reporting the shooting at John's house, cops can't be far behind. I wonder if the FBI is still investigating Margie's death.

Suddenly I remember what I meant to tell John last night, and almost did this morning. It's hard to say her name without the image of her, dead, flashing across my mind, but finally the words come out. "John. You think nobody knows about the car, but they were awfully interested in the garage and the tire tracks in the grass—"

"Yeah, I got the ones in the dirt, but forgot about the grass."

"—so maybe—Margie—did know, somehow, and what if she mentioned it to Jordan?"

"Don't worry about him," John says. "If she knew, it wasn't because I ever told her. Some things, you keep to yourself."

Like what happened with Al at the Morningbird Hotel. What almost happened.

Morningbird reminds me of my suspicion that John was there that night when I went back for my lost money. I'm wondering how to ask him when we arrive at a clearing not much bigger than the one near John's house.

While Ernie and I set up the tent, easier this time because we know the procedure, John leans against the Caddy, smoking a cigarette. When it's finished, he opens the trunk and takes out the cooler, the fishing gear, a little pump and two air mattresses. Ernie tackles the inflating like a pro.

"These things don't look very comfortable."

"Better than the ground," John points out.

"Not by much," Ernie adds. "My—"

His lips clamp shut and he reaches for one of John's cigarettes. Determined to fit in, I think. Kill himself trying.

"You fellows were lucky last night. I hadn't planned on staying in the house until I caught Jordan snooping. Just wanted to bring the album to show you."

"You packed your gun like you knew he'd be there." Ernie's taken up the questioning.

"Didn't know. Pays to be prepared. His car was parked out back, so I snuck up on the front porch and saw him through the window. He saw me, reached for my dad's rifle over the bedroom door, I shot first."

"And he shot back."

"At close range, when you're scared, a rifle's no good."

"Then you fired again."

"I had more bullets." He opens the cooler and pops the top on a beer.

My turn. "John, somebody else must know about the Caddy."

"Who?" His sharp frown draws his eyebrows together.

"Your friend who stole the money and gave it to you the other night."

Ernie gasps, and John straightens from his slouched position. Ernie accuses, "I'm not the only one with a foot-in-the-mouth problem." John demands, "How'd you know about that?"

I wiggle myself out as best I can. "We didn't know it was you at the time. We just happened to be sleeping in your garage, and later put two and two together. But, won't he tell the authorities if they question him?"

John gives the matter some thought. "He'll tell them I was driving a 1995 Olds station wagon. That car's on its way to Mexico." He laughs, lights another cigarette.

I notice Ernie's not smoking his, only holding it, knocking off the ashes every now and then. Makes me grin, and I decide I'm not mad at him for wanting to ditch me.

Mellowed, John goes on. "My so-called friend works at the credit union. Worked. He's probably been fired by now. For part of the money, he used his position to break into Jordan's safe deposit box."

"Where'd the money come from?" Ernie's back in the game, beer's more his style than smoking.

I wish for a jug of spring water and a chocolate bar. And a map, radio, cell phone, and money to spend at the festival. John can provide all those things, and more, if I stick with him.

"Jordan transferred it from the joint account he had with Margie. She got most of it from me."

"But you weren't divorced, so it wasn't a settlement."

"I wanted her to have a way out, if she ever needed it."

"And you think he killed her because he believed you and she were in the heist together."

"That's how I figure it. He might not have meant to kill her, but that was the result."

He shoves off from the car and picks up the tackle box. "You gents ready to fish?"

I want to say, She never should have put Jordan's name on her account. Ernie crooks an arm around my neck, warning-pinches me on the shoulder in the process. "Let's fish." I sense that he's read my mind again. Or maybe it's his own mind, in tune with John's, that prompts him to silence me.

It's hard for me to sympathize with the guilt they share over deeds done and undone. The only thing I can feel bad about is losing Jerry's donation to the Mouse-Runs-Away fund at the Morningbird, and that wasn't my fault. Or maybe it was, for trusting Al. Will I be sorry for trusting these two, with nothing but instinct to guide me?

So the cash in the grocery bag is John's, though he'll have a hard time proving that after it's been through two other accounts. Insurance from his mother's death, not Margie's. An inheritance from his father's estate. And John sold the house he and Margie lived in. No wonder there's a bundle, half a million by Ernie's estimation.

When we're on the stream bank casting colorful flies over the water into shady pools, I realize Ernie still thinks I'm pissed at him. He's gone downstream.

John's lounging on a boulder, drinking another beer, letting his reel idle beside him. Remembering his boyhood at the farmhouse? Thinking of Margie? Since she's been identified as his wife, he's responsible for her funeral. Unless she has family. Maybe there's already been a funeral, and he missed it.

I wind in my line and pick a path through shore debris to Ernie. "Catching anything?"

I'm amazed when he lifts a cord from the shallows and brings up three pan-sized rainbows. "Lunch," he says. "I hope you packed something to cook them in."

Now I have something to feel guilty about.

The trout smell heavenly, roasting over John's campfire. Turns out, he's bought not only a pan but a "cowboy" coffee pot as well, so we have coffee courtesy of John, fruit cups courtesy of me. No green leafies, and I'd rob a supermarket for a tomato, but settling down for a nap in the shade, we're feeling no pain.

Although how they can sleep on those air mattresses is a mystery. I'm happy with the blanket—minus the gun—spread on a carpet of thick moss, our clothes doing duty as my pillow. The tent's getting too much sun to be comfortable at this time of day.

John's reliving as much of his happy past as possible, I understand that. If leaving the sweet-sad little house gives me a twinge, multiplying it a hundredfold hints at what he must feel. Ernie said the other night that he might never go home, yet he called his dad. Maybe John and I share something, too. We're jealous of Ernie for having a dad he can call.

John's lightly snoring. I creep close to Ernie. "You awake?"

He is. "Eat too much, Mouse?"

"You kidding? That was an appetizer."

"Have some peanut butter and crackers."

105

"And a beer."

We laugh, and everything's okay between us again. Is it okay enough for me to ask what's been on my mind? I do it anyway. "Ernie. What did your dad say last night?"

I'm afraid his silence means he isn't going to answer, but at least he doesn't hit me or move away. He sits up, sifts handfuls of sand in the space between us.

"He's angry with Mother for putting up the posters. Says it makes him look like an overbearing fool, and will lose him half his clients. And if Hoodoo sees one of them, he'll take her far far from here."

So he has a mother. An idiot for a sister. And a prick for a father. "Too bad," I say, and return to my blanket.

The festival starts about 6:00, within walking distance. Traffic's roped off from the downtown with yellow tape. Rides and booths fill the main street and half a dozen side streets. Shops are open, live music's playing on a bandstand. Teens run in packs, littler kids with their parents eat popcorn and candy apples, and babies in arms, strollers, and carriers have balloons tied to their wrists.

It's exactly like the one in Hackett, which the dorm masters took us to a couple of years ago. I remember having fun, but something happened that finished such excursions. We Middles speculated long about what made O'Leary lay down the law, but we never found out for sure. I think one of the Almost-Outs got away. Could be that's why they're so close-mouthed about my vanishing act.

Ernie and I wander among the vendors' booths. Paintings, fancy pillows, carvings, jewelry, even clothing. Cotton candy, Greek pastries, cartons of spicy noodles, tacos. At some point I look around and I'm alone. After a dart of fear, I remember John's given me ten dollars, so I try to find something healthful.

I end up on the court house square, seated on a rock wall too close to a country band, eating a burger. Apparently it's the only thing going that has lettuce—and a slice of tomato so thin I could read a book through it.

Ernie emerges from the milling crowd with a sack in each arm. One is full of farm-fresh tomatoes and ear corn, leaf lettuce, slices of homemade bread, and small containers of slaw. The other has buttered baked potatoes in foil, and squares of fudge wrapped in plastic. Real fudge, with walnuts. He's been down a side street I missed.

"Where's John?"

I shake my head, my mouth already full of tomato. Juice runs down my chin and onto my 'Cute Kid' t-shirt.

"You're supposed to make a sandwich," he laughs.

"I already had bread."

He uses his pocket knife to slice another tomato and fixes himself a sandwich. When we've gorged ourselves and tossed the potato foil at one of the overflowing trash cans, John finds us and adds a bottled drink to the picnic.

"Omigosh, I can't believe it. How did you know?" He's handed me a grape fizzy, something I haven't had since that last foster home. East Wind frowns on carbonated drinks.

He grins "One of the flavors of childhood."

"Yeah," I say, "like cotton candy." The glass enclosed cart with its paper cones topped with fluffy pink was the first thing I saw that I wanted, but jolting my system on pure sugar hadn't seemed smart. Fudge and a purple drink later, it's even less smart, and I regret missing that childhood flavor.

Munching on the sandwich Ernie makes for him, John sits on the rock wall as if in a trance. It's the first time I've seen him this far away from the Caddy in the clearing. He's far away from us, too.

After another half hour, the sky's dark, the crowd's breaking up, and a voice comes over the loudspeaker. "Fireworks in ten minutes, folks. Meet you at the fairgrounds."

Trolley-style buses are loading at the corners of the square. "Too late for cotton candy now." We carry what we haven't eaten and board one. It takes us around the taped-off area and out of town to a long sloping grassy field where folks have spread blankets and quilts.

Lacking a blanket or quilt, we lie on the grass. It's thick and dry, and the fireworks are fine. Rockets soar and burst into showers of color and puffs of smoke. None of that earsplitting thunder that scares dogs into convulsions, but elaborate designs that must have cost the town plenty.

The show lasts longer than the ones I remember. During the pause that comes right before the finale, I lean over and say in Ernie's ear, "This is the best night of my life."

There's a terrific surge as the rest of the fireworks shoot up up up up and begin exploding all over the inky sky.

Then I swear, I hear a gun go off.

I turn around to find out whether John, behind us, heard it too.

Episode 14

He's not there.

I scan the crowds of people moving in all directions, mostly toward the parking lot, but in the dim glow from a few flashlights and fewer headlights, I can tell we've been abandoned again.

"Did you hear that shot?" I ask Ernie, who by now is looking around too with his hands propped on his hips, annoyed. "Think he's in trouble?"

"I heard something. But it didn't come from the campsite. It's that way." He gestures over a cluster of fairground buildings on a little knoll.

Ernie's sense of direction is another of his many talents, and I'm impressed, though not exactly convinced and certainly not reassured. "What should we do?" The trolleys are leaving and I want to be on one. Wherever the campsite is, getting to it will be quicker if we follow the route we came in on. My enthusiasm for trekking over that wooded knoll in the dark and maybe without a path, is zero.

He picks up our bag of leftover groceries and starts across the grass. Everyone's flowing toward the exit, and some cars are already lined up to get onto the single dirt road to the highway. Trolleys bully their way into position, and we're able to grab seats on the first, right behind the driver.

"Where could he be?" My thoughts are stuck in that groove, with a side trip into, What is he doing? And why? Did he always intend to leave us here while he disappeared into the night, bent on fulfilling his secret mission? Or did he see someone in the crowd and run?

"You'd better hope he turns up at camp, because that's where we're going to spend the night. Hope the tent's there, if nothing else. We don't have money for a motel, or hotel, or whatever this burg's got in the way of accommodations."

"Was that really a gunshot? Or do I just have guns on the brain?"

"In the morning we'll get a paper and see if the cops arrested anybody for having too much fun at the festival."

"Or some farmer shooting at a chicken thi—"

"Hey, Jason, you're leaving one," comes a voice from the back of the trolley. Heads crane around and as we move into the turn I spot John running after us. He's silhouetted by car lights, carrying something in one hand and waving the other. Three somethings, the size and shape of microwave popcorn bags.

We're a few hundred yards from the highway and our driver isn't slowing down. "He can take one of the other trolleys," Jason calls over his shoulder.

"Ernie, that's John!"

Ernie stands up, leans close to Jason, holds something against the man's neck. "Stop the damn bus," he says. Low, calm. Scary.

We careen over to the shoulder and brake to a neck-snapping halt. Squeals and babble from other passengers, a mix of surprise and approval, some laughter. Hands reach out and help John aboard. In the fleeting glow of car lights, he pauses, uncertain. "Ernie? You guys here?"

"Here we are!" I cry, and he makes his way along an aisle full of feet. Ernie steps aside and John swings onto the seat with me. "You run pretty good for an old man," Ernie jokes. John quips, "Checking the other trolleys slowed me down." Now that we're together, it's easy to think he'd only been visiting one of the portable toilets. I decide to work on curbing my imagination.

John's breathing is normal by the time we hit the first traffic light into town.

I'm not prepared for what he says.

"Why'd you take off like that? I wasn't gone more than ten minutes. You better be glad I found you, because I have the flashlight."

Ernie says mildly, "You could have told us you were going, and we'd've waited."

"I wanted it to be a surprise." He gives me one of the puffy round plastic bags.

Passing under fitful street lights, I hold up the clear bag but still can't tell what's inside. Ernie opens his, pulls out a bunch of something and pops it into my mouth.

"Cotton candy!" At first there's a thrill as the sweetness melts over my tongue and I'm in third grade, watching a vendor twirl the pink threads over a paper cone, taking my first bite, getting it all over my face.

It's not as exciting, wadded into a bag, but every bit as tasty. I've finished about a third of it when a wave of emotion sweeps over me and the next thing I know I'm blubbering. Ernie politely ignores me, John lays a hand on my shoulder, and I duck my head into a shadow and pretend to be coughing.

The driver stops the trolley at the corner of the court house square, where we got on, and the lights are so bright I feel like I'm on a stage. "You okay?" John lets the other passengers file past. When the last few clank down the metal step, the driver turns to us and tells Ernie, "Don't you ever pull a gun on me again, dude."

110

"You brought that gun!" John sounds outraged.

Ernie holds up a small pen light. Flashes it in Jason's face.

Mid-cough I burst into laughter, tears still dripping off my chin.

Jason glares at us and makes a shooing motion with his hand. "Get off."

We do. John's mega light leading the way, we cross the two lane, into the woods. "You'd've ended up in the swamp, trying to navigate with that dinky thing."

"Served a better purpose," Ernie counters.

He's using his little light to keep from walking on my heels. Brambles clutch at my elbows and ankles, and I'm ready for an air mattress. But when we're still pretty far from the clearing, John switches off his light. Ernie kills his, too.

We stand motionless, listening.

"Stay here," John whispers near my ear and we wait while he scouts ahead. I'm surprised by how silently he can move. Was he in the military, or just a squirrel or deer hunter? He's comfortable with handguns, and his dad owned a rifle. Which Jordan took with him.

John's gone a long time. My fears return, with that confusion of yearning and regret for things I can't define. Tears well up, spill over, and I blow my nose on my t-shirt.

"What's the matter with you?" Ernie's voice is curious, but with an edge of impatience.

"I don't know." To steady myself, I stuff the rest of the cotton candy into my mouth.

John comes down the path, light bobbing, and says, "All clear."

We follow him into camp and he breaks out a fresh six-pack. "Just what I need," I tell Ernie. "A sugar high multiplied by alcohol content."

"You don't have to drink it," he tells me. "We're not putting a gun to your head."

I fall over laughing and at first he doesn't realize what's funny. Then he flashes the pen light into my eyes and we scuffle a bit, spilling beer from both cans. He knuckles my head. "That's the second time you've done that."

John regards us with a smile. "Better get some sleep. We'll be up early."

Stumbling toward the tent, I strip off my t-shirt, cruddy with dried tomato juice, wet snot, and now a smelly dose of beer. The two air mattresses fill the space, a blanket spread over each. Behind me Ernie says, "John's going to sleep in the Caddy."

Off come the ragged sneakers. I dump them and the shirt beside the tent and crawl in. After John shuts off the mega light, there's silence and darkness and nothing moves. For about a minute I believe I'm sleeping. Then I hear Ernie taking a leak on the other side of the nylon. I hope he isn't pissing into my shoes.

The open flap at the back lets in a cooling breeze and the occasional soft hoot of an owl somewhere deep in woods too thick for a glimpse of civilization. Trucks pass on the highway, and faint cheerful conversation and the drone of a distant radio turn my thoughts to the festival and the fact that I have over seven dollars left of the money John gave me.

If we go into town tomorrow, I'll buy a pair of tennies at some discount place or thrift store. Maybe find a camera that my cartridge will fit and I can finish taking up the roll.

Ernie tosses restlessly beside me and I wonder what's on his mind. Fran, for sure. What else? Is he reliving our adventures, like I am? Wishing he was home, like I'm not. But I do wish we were in the sad farmhouse, sleeping in the twin beds without any threat of intruders.

Then I know what turned me into a sniveling crybaby on the trolley. Until John handed me that cotton candy, I still had doubts about him, and because I was having such a good time playing the fugitive with him, I'd given little thought to what he must be feeling. My head knew he was desperate, yet what he'd told us, what I'd seen with my own eyes and heard on the news, hadn't really touched me before.

But the moment I tasted the treat he'd gone out of his way to give me, I knew he was innocent, and my heart filled with sorrow for him. Playing fugitive was one thing, being one was another. 'They think you did it,' the friend who stole the money for him had said the other night.

And on top of that, while he was doing something nice for us, we'd gone off and left him. Did he feel like us, then? Abandoned, not knowing what to do. I can still see him running to catch up, hear his panting question, 'You guys here?'

"Can't sleep, Mouse?"

I confess, "I figured out why I acted like a dork over the candy."

Ernie confesses, "I had a defining moment like that last night."

Sitting up, I try to read his face, but the waning moon's not co-operating. "What was it?"

"When he showed us the album. You didn't look at those pictures of all the stuff that came with that car, did you. Girly stuff, like a mirror and nail file and perfume, meant for a rich woman or a rich man's wife. I had to wonder what John's mother thought of it. And when the car came to him through his dad's estate, he never told Margie. He put the accessories in a box and kept it in the farmhouse basement. Guess it's still there."

I want more than ever to go back and live in that house, discover all its secrets.

When I do sleep, I dream, and my dream is not of John's house, or his car, or his dead wife. I know I'm dreaming but I can't wake up. I'm in the foster home, hauling a giant vacuum cleaner through a maze of rooms. The floors are made of river bank sand, and the cleaner keeps falling apart. I'm so mad I'm crying, but if I make a run for freedom I'll be caught and punished, so I keep putting the pieces together and guide the nozzle over the sand, which is endless.

"What the hell IS that?" Ernie sits up, groggy and wild-haired.

'That' is John, using a hand vac to clean up the sand we've tracked onto the Caddy's carpet.

Remorse sweeps over me again but I don't cry. Instead, I go and take the vac from him. By the time the job's completed, he's made coffee and Ernie's roasting the corn ears in a bed of ashes raked to one side of the fire.

"Corn for breakfast?"

John says, "You eat corn flakes, don't you?"

"Those don't look very flaky." They're still in the husks, which are brownish-gray from ashes and heat. Mixed with the aroma of coffee, they smell marvelous. I hunker near Ernie. "How do you know when they're done?"

He glances sideways at me with a little grin. Together we say, "Another one of your/my many talents." Then he explains, "Boy Scouts. Long time ago."

While we're scarfing down breakfast, John asks, "You want to swim, or shower in the campground wash house?"

There's a campground? "Shower!" we both shout. I hope it's not one of the ultra primitive ones I've read about with stinky pit toilets and no hot water and black mold growing on everything.

Ernie surprises me . Instead of packing that paper bag full of clothes, he's also brought two towels, soap, toothpaste and toothbrushes, and dental floss. "Crikey, you really ARE a Boy Scout. Always prepared. Ready for anything."

His mood goes somber. "Not always."

John points us onto the faint footpath that winds through undergrowth topped by pine forest. In about ten minutes we come out right behind the campground wash house. At this time of morning it's deserted and we get our pick of showers in a clean, tiled, brightly lit facility.

The bar soap Ernie hands me has a manly, antibacterial scent, and the water's adjustable to my temperature. Happily, I wash myself and the dirty clothes I've had the foresight to bring along. A hundred times better than East Wind. When I finally shut off the spray because my fingers are wrinkly, I'm squeaky clean outside and completely contented inside. Dry and dressed in my other outfit, I'm prepared for anything.

Ernie and I step through the plastic curtain and into cooler air at the same time. He's letting his beard grow, and only a pair of brown leather sandals is needed to transform him from the clean-cut corporate son into a free-wheeling campus rebel.

"Let's buy some foot gear today," I suggest, flossing the corn out of my teeth. "I have enough money and I bet John would give you more."

He towels his curly hair thoughtfully. "I have money."

My eyebrows ask a question and he completes the explanation. "But I can't get to it for two more months."

John's right, then. "So how rich are you?"

I've never known a rich person, but I've seen full page color photos of the high life in magazines. Mansions in Beverly Hills and New York on tv. Palaces in books, and in my dreams. What I can't picture is Ernie in any of them.

"Mother set up a trust fund for me the week I was born. Nobody can touch it until my eighteenth birthday."

"Eighteen. Just in time for college."

"University."

"Figures."

We sit on adjacent wood benches as he re-packs items in my duffel bag. The wet towels and clothes will have to dry on bushes at our campsite.

"It's a long, convoluted mess. When Fran was old enough to realize that all of Mom's inheritance was going to be mine, she freaked. Didn't matter that the deal was done before she was born. Her resentment drove Mom to leave us two years ago. Didn't help that Dad gave the kid everything she wanted and more. Then sometime around last Christmas, Fran met Hoodoo and everything went to hell."

"And you're trying to bring it all back to—what? The same convoluted mess it was before Hoodoo?"

The sound he makes isn't amused. "Not trying any more." He goes to one of the mirrors and starts combing his hair.

At the next sink, I load paste on my toothbrush, pause to say, "But you love Fran. Isn't she worth—"

115

His reflected eyes meet my stare. "Love her? I can't stand her."

Episode 15

Did I hear that right?

Those glowing images Ernie put in my head—traveling with Fran and Hoodoo in the first place, pleading at the abandoned gas station when she blew him off and didn't choose him even after Hoodoo slugged him, his faded memories triggered by a little white sandal in the Haw Creek school infirmary, the way his voice cracked when he told me about her following him around wanting him to read to her, his face when he saw her photo on the Missing Child poster—ended abruptly with his words, "I can't stand her."

I don't know what to say, so I finish brushing my teeth and reach for the comb. He doesn't say anything either, but when he gives it to me, I feel tense vibes coming off him like radiation and I step away to keep from being burned.

He finds extra toilet paper rolls in an overhead cabinet in the corner, and stuffs three on top of the other items in my duffel bag. Ever the practical guy.

On the path, him marching ahead, me bringing up the rear, I wonder when it will be safe to speak. Then he says, "None of it was Mom's fault, but she's the one taking the brunt."

No, I think. You are.

"You don't live with her? You stayed with Fran and your dad?"

"When he was granted custody—unfairly, because he's a prime manipulator—all she got was visitation. I see her on my birthday."

"In two months."

"Yeah," Ernie says, without emotion. He's stuck in the past, but I think of the future.

Eighteen, the magic number. Ernie will officially be a man, and in four years and three months I'll be walking out of East Wind forever.

Then it dawns on me: I'm out now. The question is, for how long. I want to go into town, but the chance that my mug actually is on a wanted poster—and some citizen might recognize me—is greater than whether a grownup like John will be remembered from his childhood.

"Aaahh!"

"What?" Ernie turns, puzzled and maybe put on guard by my exclamation.

"John wanted to be a kid again at the festival before leaving the country."

Ernie teasingly messes up my hair. "You just figure that out?"

We tramp through the last few yards of underbrush to the familiar clearing. So the plan is to flee. Excited, I'm swept into the whole fugitive thing again, but with a deeper understanding of the guys I'm fleeing with.

John's giving up his home place and the probability that he can clear his name. Ernie's giving up attending university and a better relationship with his mother.

All I'm giving up is some doubtful friendships and an excellent education. Being a minor, I'm facing a worse place than East Wind if I'm taken into custody with these two. Or East Wind at its worst if I'm returned, which is unlikely after they let me escape.

What will we do in another country? How do they intend to handle the border red tape? My companions are inventive and capable, and my confidence soars with eagerness to experience whatever's ahead.

John's gone into town already—or swiped it from a camper—because he's reading a newspaper. He looks up, watches us spread the wet things. His hair's wet, too, so he's been swimming in the river one last time. Alone. Dangerous. There are deep pools and the water's swift in the middle.

"I need running shoes," I say. "And if Ernie's going to disguise himself as a poet, he should have a pair of brown leather sandals."

They look at me with surprise and amusement. "Easy enough," John tells us.

"Actually, I had sandals," Ernie says. "They're in the SUV."

We don't go there. Instead we wash the coffee pot and cups at the edge of a backwater. But mentioning the SUV prompts me to wonder where Hoodoo and Fran are. Is Jordan out of the hospital yet? And is Bob the Reporter still with Martin the Cuz, or is he pursuing the story of the runaway scandal at East Wind?

Ernie breaks the comfortable silence with, "John, we should pack up. There's details that need to be taken care of."

"Yeah, we will. First, look at this."

'This' is below-the-fold news in a small town daily, so when I do see my face in gray pixels, it doesn't bother me the way I'd expected. It's an old school photo, but clear enough that I won't be buying my shoes in Glen Alpine.

"Pity you can't grow a mustache," Ernie jokes. He reads the article aloud and there's not much there. I can imagine kids my age being stopped by cops all across the country.

Then I notice the name attached to the report. Robert. Good ol' Bob. If he didn't know me in the farmhouse, he will the next time he sees me. My eyes meet Ernie's. "Yep. Time to hit the road."

Focused on touching base with his past, John never asked who the visitors were that sent him flying yesterday morning, so we fill him in about the Suits, Bob and Martin. He heaves a sigh. "That's not good. I was counting on Ernie driving, but now he's a target too."

"Maybe, maybe not. Let's buy the kid some decent shoes, and we can discuss other stuff later."

"Not in this town," I remind him. "It's my picture in the paper."

"Three sitting ducks," Ernie observes. "Time for drastic measures."

John starts packing up the cooking gear, cooler, and empty beer cans. Ernie and I roll up blankets and deflate the mattresses. We un-pitch the tent and force it into its storage bag. In half an hour, only dry ashes can reveal that anyone's been there. No stray cigarette butts, no footprints, and as soon as Ernie moves the Caddy to rocky ground, no tire tracks. John's methodical and thorough. Just like Ernie. I vow to watch and learn, and be just like them.

We get in the Caddy. Instead of asking 'Where to?' Ernie announces, "I know a couple of guys who can help."

He guides the car back the way we came, and when the Interstate is before us he heads in the same direction we were going before. Away from Glen Alpine, away from everywhere I've ever been and toward the unknown.

Fifteen minutes of countryside later, John says, "What can they help with?"

"First things first," Ernie tells him.

I'm surprised Ernie's taking charge like this. Dumfounded that John's letting him. Maybe the denial, anger, guilt, and whatever the other stages of grief are, have worked their way out of his system and he's too numb to object. I'm too happy to worry about it.

After two boring hours of radio, silence, more radio, silence, and a patchwork of fields, signs for towns I never heard of, woods, fields, and more signs, we finally pass one that's a relief to us all: 'Rest Area 3 miles.'

Not caring to remember the other rest areas I've had the ill-luck to visit, I run into the building before anyone can stop me with any cautions. Rested, I meet them strolling along, grinning. John gives me money and I buy some cola and a pack of peanuts. While they're inside, I dawdle on a bench, sharing with a squirrel, and wonder what they're saying to each other. If the last hundred miles is any gauge, it's not much.

Oops. They come out together, arguing.

John pokes Ernie's shoulder with a forefinger, hard enough to hurt. "Forget it! It ain't gonna happen."

Ernie buys himself a drink and a pack of cheese crackers. Sits on the bench beside me.

John goes to the Caddy, parked as near behind some bushes as Ernie could put it, but not on the sidewalk or grass where it might draw the attention of an attendant. I expect him to get in the driver's seat, but he doesn't.

"Still won't let you paint her?"

"Have I said that she sticks out like an old maid on a basketball court?"

"Probably. But as long as we've left the Suits behind, what does it matter? They're the only ones who can connect you to me or John."

"At the moment, that's true. Things have a way of changing."

"He'll come around. When he has to."

"Maybe. First, a couple of other stops."

"You know where you are, then."

"Yep."

I look around me with more interest. If Ernie's in his home territory, is he going to say goodbye to his dad, or find his mom, or drive by his house and I'll see where he lives. What's around me right now is just a shady pit stop on the Interstate, though, and maybe we're miles from his destination.

Neither of them says a word when we return to the car, and Ernie keeps heading west.

The sun's still behind when we exit at a dusty collection of shacks and rows of tables stretching for maybe half a mile in what apparently used to be a pasture on the other side of an access road from the four-lane. Ernie parks in an almost-illegal space, way down on the end of a line of cars on the grass, under some trees.

"Not pines," John tells him. "Took me an hour this morning washing the goo of campground pines off her."

It's a flea market and I have high hopes for finding a camera.

We find plenty of other stuff, too, mostly useless, but Ernie picks up a new cowboy hat and a belt with a gaudy silver buckle (kind of like mine) and a really classy pair of boots made of soft leather. "Black market," he says, but buys them anyway. With a small wad of John's money. John's wearing oversized silver sunglasses and a ball cap, and loads up a paper bag with fruit and vegetables we can eat without cooking.

I'm looking for running shoes when I spot a whole table full of cameras, and buy one that my cartridge works in for only five bucks. I test it by ratcheting the film and taking a couple shots of the old guy who sold it to me.

It's refreshing to have money and things to look forward to besides swimming every day in the East Wind pool, and listening to Steve tootle on his clarinet and Jerry bitch about his chores. The only thing I really miss is the library.

Finding a book stall, I fill a plastic bag with paperbacks. One of them is an S.E. Hinton I've never read. My life is complete.

Well, no. No shoes yet, though there are plenty to choose from. They're all either too big, too small, or too heavy for summer wear. I'm about to sink a couple dollars into new tennies when Ernie calls me over.

"Here's what you need." He hands me a pair, navy and white, lightweight and streamlined. I try them on and agree. Money exchanges hands. "I could use another t-shirt. I was wearing this one when I went over the wall."

"This would be better." Ernie holds up a frilly pink dress and a curly black wig. "They'll never think to look for a girl."

He laughs as he tries to set the wig on my head. I dodge and we scuffle. He drapes the dress over my face. I try to fight it off without ripping it. You rip, you pay.

We're laughing like crazy when John hurries up to us, not exactly scared, but tense. "Couple of cops." He nods and we both look.

Shaved heads, khaki creased enough to cut you, polished and loaded down with stuff on their belts. Walkie-talkie, cell phone, pager, handcuffs. Guns.

They're talking to the old guy who sold me the camera. Hugging my bag of purchases, I sprint around a canvas booth, John on my heels with our groceries.

Jogging along a dirt driveway behind the line of vendors, we're probably drawing more attention than if we'd sauntered away like Ernie's doing, carrying his running shoes, my worn-out sneaks, and a guitar he's picked up somewhere. Guitar? And I thought he was disguised as Richard Petty.

We make it to the car without a tail, and in a few minutes he catches up to us and slides into the driver's seat. Something's been nagging at me for a couple of days, and I just now realize what it is. The car doesn't have seat belts. I point that out, adding, "What if a highway patrol pulls us over?"

"Vintage cars don't need belts," Ernie assures me.

Yeah. Right. And the first time we're stopped and asked for driver's license and registration, will they hand it over? That move would land us in cuffs or set us off on a cross-country chase. Seeing those cops has started my worry cycle again, like the dryer that used to sound off like a train horn when the permanent press was ready to quit, but the tub kept turning anyway, and if you didn't take the clothes out, the churning would continue for a few minutes until you forgot about it and then the horn would blast you out of your daydream, and Whatever-her-name-was would yell, "Get the damn things NOW, Vinnie."

Wherever I end up, I hope I don't have to do the laundry.

After another hour, Ernie zooms up an off-ramp which either wasn't marked or I wasn't paying attention. We drive through an industrial area, then a residential area, then a seedy old downtown outskirts area to a public parking garage.

John comes out of his trance. "Where the hell are you taking us?"

In the rear-view I see Ernie's closed smile. Then he says, "Ever hear of the Cayman Islands?"

Episode 16

"Is that somewhere near the Canary Islands?" I'm sure it isn't. Where it IS, though, could be the way it sounds: tropical.

Sky so blue it hurts your eyes, surf so clear you can see the bottom for a mile out. Coral reefs with fish tank fish in the wild and seaweed waving in spears of sunlight. Palms swaying in sea breezes and clean white sand under bare feet. Coconut everything, drinks, desserts, coating shrimp like the dish I once had at a Red Lobster for my birthday. Paradise.

Or, it could be one of those bits of rocky land off the coast of Maine or Nova Scotia. I wish now I'd paid more attention in geography class.

Ernie laughs. John says, "I don't know about you guys, but I'm heading to Canada."

Not so you'd notice. We've been going west for what feels like three days. Might run across Hoodoo and Fran again after all. I never doubted he'd end up in California, though Ernie's taunt about being in a horror movie probably wasn't far off base.

"It's not where we're heading, exactly. Only, the money is."

John's head snaps around and he gives Ernie an astonished look. "You're kidding."

"It'll be safer there than it is in a bag."

Ernie drives the Caddy into a bank parking lot. The place is swarming. John's breathless with disbelief. "Oh, my God." He scoots down in the seat and pulls the ball cap visor as low as he can.

"We have to do this," Ernie tells him. "It's Friday and waiting till Monday could be a mistake."

"Going in would be a mistake, and what the hell do you mean by parking in the open?"

Ernie gets out. "Come on, John. We're three hundred miles from—" He stops.

We know what he means. Home. The place where everything bad happened, and where we can never go again.

"Do I stay with the car?"

"No, Mouse, you come with us."

I grab my S. E. Hinton book to read in the lobby. Ernie opens the trunk and places the paper bag full of money in John's care. On the way inside, I hear Ernie say, "You have a friend at the credit union. I have one at the bank. He'll fix you up with a new life."

John recoils with surprise and almost walks into the edge of the glass door. Instead of lining up with about fifty other people doing banking on their lunch hour, Ernie signs in on a sheet like he's made an appointment. I weigh myself on an old fashioned scale and I've lost four pounds. Suddenly I'm starving and try to take my mind off food by picking a fake leather chair where I can begin reading.

Half a book later, the lunch bunch is gone and I'm alone. The Caddy's alone too. Like an old maid on a basketball court.

Voices approach along the carpeted hall. My buddies, with a pleasant-looking man in a rumpled shirt and wide tie. They stop in front of an office, he shakes John's hand, calls him 'Mister Baker.' Ernie shakes the man's hand, thanks him. He goes into the office and they come toward me.

Ernie gives John the car key. "I need to make a couple of calls. Move around to the back if you want to."

He wants to, ASAP. From where he parks, away from the street, I can see Ernie at a pay phone. I wish I'd stayed with him, maybe find out who he's talking to, but somehow I didn't quite trust John not to leave us.

Friday. The day I was supposed to call Jerry and Steve and tell them I'd found a job in Dentonville and earned enough money to book a motel room for them. I wonder whether they ever really expected me to do that, or it was all just a prank to get me in trouble with old Collins and his boss O'Leary.

In less than a week, I've lived more in the real world than in my whole life before. Which could be more interesting, sharing John's new life, or digging into Ernie's old one? If we stay together, I can do both.

"We may be here a few days," Ernie tells us when he comes back. He's picked up a map in the bank, and adds, "Better let me drive."

Sun's bright, sky's clear, leaves are almost to their full summer growth already. Instead of touring the town, which appears to be larger than the ones we've been in so far, Ernie takes us through a maze of residential streets and finally out on a curving by-pass. We hit a stretch of empty shopping centers, closed car dealership, little places still open but dying.

A traffic light stops us.

In the next block, a small run-down motel makes my heart flutter. He flicks on the turn signal. My mouth goes dry. At least it's one level, no fire escape, and the sign's readable.

'Starshine.' Bulbs around the name form a star, and I make a mental note to see how many of them come on after dark.

We drive around to the back and he parks close to the building. He and John look at each other. "I'll go," Ernie volunteers. "Nobody's looking for me."

Definitely the best thing going for us. But the way he says those words hurts me.

All those people in his family, and he's as alone as we are. I want to tell him, having the orphan police after you is no picnic, but he's rounding the corner of the motel to the office. John says softly, "Not yet, anyway."

"Ernie's smart." The only thing he hasn't excelled at is running a carpet sweeper. I clamp my lips shut against listing out loud, not in any order, what he can do.

Find shelter, avoid detection, pick locks, soothe skinned skin, repair a lawn mower, convince grown men he's a tough teen, grill a mean burger. Catch and cook fish, remember to pack dental floss, pretend not to notice embarrassing moments. Joke around like a regular guy instead of a rich brat. Navigate from memory or a map. He can stand up to people, drive a heavy old car in impossible places, pull strings to create a new life for the three of us. Oh, and make coffee.

He couldn't do the one thing he set out to accomplish, though. Persuade Francine to wise up and go home. I wonder what kind of hold Hoodoo has on her, that Ernie can't break.

Seeing him returning, we get out of the Caddy. He hands John a room receipt and a key. "We're here, you're there." The rooms are next to each other, opening on this parking lot.

John reads what he's written in the blanks, and laughs.

"When you're settled in, Mister Baker, come on over for lunch." Ernie carries in the bag of veggies. I take the bedroll and my duffel. Ernie goes back for his new guitar.

"Can you play that thing?" I leap onto the nearest bed and test the mattress and pillow. Thick and thin, the way I like them. The sheets and even the blanket smell clean, a relief.

"Later," he tells me. He checks the bathroom and brings in the toilet paper from the campground. There's no phone book, and we find the tv remote under my bed. There is an ice bucket which has seen better days. "No liner, no cups. Better get some drinks. Machines are in the covered walkway." He gestures.

I pass John's open door. He's standing at the foot of his bed, staring into his suitcase. Missing that bag of money. Wondering what he's gotten himself into. I grin. Welcome to the club.

Our lunch of tomatoes, cucumbers, and carrots is an almost-salad. Cut up with Ernie's knife, it's finger food. No lettuce, dressing, peppers, or onions.

John clicks on the tv and I'm amazed. Not only does it work, it has about three hundred channels and they all come in clear. He quickly switches away from a commercial advertising a local steak house. News, he shuts off.

I fill in my hollow spaces with junk food from the candy machine. Open my book to where I left off. Ernie gathers up our lunch trash, and John goes back to his room for a nap.

"He's in bad shape," I venture. "Lost his spunk."

Ernie stretches out on his bed. When you're on the run, you sleep every chance you get. "Haven't we all."

I haven't. I'm happier than I've been in . . . Ever.

It's still early—well, daylight, anyway—when John knocks. He's carrying a phone book and announces, "I'm going to call out for pizza. Place your orders."

"Pepperoni," I shout. Ernie votes for a veggie. Figures. John wants sausage. Three mediums should be enough to share and gorge half the night.

He comes back and says they won't deliver a pitcher of beer, so we bring more soft drinks from the machine. While we wait for the food, John gives the tv another try. The news sounds weird, since all of the anchors and weathermen are unfamiliar. "You know any of these people?" I ask Ernie, meaning, 'Are they the ones on tv at your home?' but the pizzas arrive so he avoids answering.

John mutes the sound so we can eat in peace, and we trade slices so everybody is satisfied with the selection. It's my idea of perfect pizza—thin crust, medium cheese, and plenty of tomato sauce. While we're stuffing our faces and guzzling soda, we glimpse a silent kaleidoscope of crying mothers and cop cars racing about, groups of citizens at some meeting, others carrying signs and demonstrating, kids and animals being rescued. Stock market report, ads for tire stores.

Then a Special Bulletin. Our chewing stops. We watch John's wedding photo flash to the front. Margie, alive. Happy. It zooms to a fraction of the screen and hovers over the head of some guy whose mouth moves, saying things John doesn't want to hear.

"Find out where they're looking," Ernie suggests quietly.

John presses the button and the announcer trails off with, ". . . wanted for questioning. If you have any information, please call the number at the bottom of your screen." The news guy repeats the number twice, and someone else at the station starts waving his arm over a weather map.

"He's reporting from Dentonville," Ernie says. "Not to worry."

John doesn't say anything. He leaves the last few slices of his pizza, drains the drink can, takes a cigarette pack from his shirt pocket. Outside, he paces, smoke trailing him.

Ernie perches on the edge of the single plastic chair and starts tuning his guitar. He looks like he knows what he's doing. It's unamplified, and he has a simple pick, not the kind you fit over your fingers, but the kind you lose the first time you turn around. Steve once told us his uncle used to play 'She'll be Comin' Round the Mountain' and Jerry made a vulgar joke.

Ernie's tune is pretty. John must not think so, because he yells, "Good night," and disappears into the evening gloom.

"Margie's favorite," I remark.

"Fran's."

"You can't stand her."

"I like the song."

"What is it?"

"Moon River."

I sit on my bed, kick off my new shoes. He's playing softly, but hears me when I go on. "That's why you didn't mess with the blonde in the red car. She made you think of Fran."

He doesn't miss a beat, doesn't look up. "Yep."

Flipping channels, I come across a bunch of nearly naked women dancing around in a basement. He motions me to give up the remote and shuts off the whole thing. I snap on the bedside lamp and finish my book. The ending's tragic and I toss it away.

The weatherman predicted hotter temperatures tomorrow. Using Ernie's knife, I rip off the legs of my thrift shop jeans at the knee. Turn my East Wind t-shirt so the logo's on the inside. Remember the wig and dress, and try to think of some prank to pull on Ernie. One that doesn't end up with my foot in my mouth.

After we're settled in, everything's dark except for a faint glow outside from a distant street light way down past the end of the building. Cool air circulates between the tiny bathroom window and the front door. A patter of rain reminds me of Haw Creek, except tonight I'm not drunk and my scabby knees and elbows and chin have peeled and healed.

It's a lot like camping in the tent, but more comfortable, and I should be sleeping, but too much food and caffeine, memories and questions, keep me awake. Ernie's snoring gently. He might be alone except for us, but that's not interfering with his rest.

I remember one of the drink machines has juice, coffee, and chocolate milk. Feeling in my jeans pocket, I come up with enough change.

A step over the threshold, I'm startled by the shape of someone sitting in the Caddy and I duck back, then lean to peer through the cascade of water on the windshield. Whoever is behind the wheel doesn't move. For a long while, nothing. Only the rain, Ernie's snoring, and an occasional gust of night wind.

John gets out, locks the car. Goes into his room. I breathe a long sigh. No Suit, planting a bomb. No cop looking for clues. No danger.

The walkway is cold and damp under my bare feet. The window to John's room is open, curtains closed, the light over his door is out, just like ours. I hurry to the brightly lit machines and pay for a couple containers of chocolate milk. While drinking the first one, I count bulbs in this side of the motel sign. Two of the starfish arms look chopped off, blending into the night sky behind them. Seedy or not, I love it.

Inside again, I slip the chain lock into place. Open our window. Drink the second milk in the dark. Get into bed without brushing my teeth, and smile on the way to sleep.

The tv news wakes me. Sound's turned so low I can barely hear it. Dressed, Ernie sits on the foot of his bed, watching the same clip about John replay. I keep quiet, waiting to see what he'll do. He watches firemen put out a house fire, and shots of a car wrapped around a telephone pole. Does he expect to see Francine? She wasn't on either of my milk cartons from last night.

"What's for breakfast?" I ask, to distract him from such thoughts, if he's thinking them.

He shuts off the tv. "Leftover pizza."

"John sleeping in?"

"It's early. Just after seven."

The machines dispense coffee, but I want mine in a mug, not paper or plastic. "Where's the phone book?"

"Nearest breakfast is ten blocks away."

"You really know this area, don't you." And me, I think.

"Yeah."

I wait for him to tell me more, but he picks up the guitar and plays a sad melody I don't recognize. "What's that?"

"My own composition."

"Does it have a name?"

His eyes dart a warning into mine, so I guess he calls it 'Francine.' With only two years separating them in age, they must have bonded at some point, in a way I never did with any of the foster kids who lived in the places I stayed.

If I have brothers or sisters, I'm not aware of them. I'd be the oldest, probably. Someday, maybe I'll go on a talk show and make a crying appeal and be reunited with people I once knew but have nothing in common with anymore.

Yeah. Sure.

"Where'd you go last night?" His question from left field surprises me.

"To the machines. And to count the star bulbs in the sign."

"Big night out, huh?" He grins. Lays aside the guitar.

"John was sitting in the Caddy. Maybe deciding to let you paint her after all."

Ernie leaps to his feet. The color's drained from his face, and that scares me. He jerks the knob but the chain holds.

"What's the matter?" I hover behind him, reaching to close the door and free the chain.

"He's got another key!"

Before he can run outside, I pull back the curtain. The parking lot is empty.

Episode 17

Ernie strides in circles on the tarmac in his underwear and screeches, "Damn! I should have known!"

His fists clench like he wants to hit something. Or someone. Guilt over not telling him last night keeps me out of range, uncertain what to do to stop his unraveling.

I think of a few things I could say but they're all pointless. John's reason for taking off at this stage in the game is anybody's guess. I'm guessing it has to do with Ernie insisting on disguising the Caddy, though Margie's photo on the news last night sure upset him. And with his new identity and the money in a secret account, what's to keep him here?

Ernie's going on and on about trust and honor and his own stupidity, when the car hoves around the building and slides to a smooth stop in the parking space. John gives us a look that says he's aware of the situation and is amused.

"Breakfast is served," he says with what he probably thinks is a British accent.

I help with the warm paper bags and we decide to eat in his room for a change. He's brought ham and egg muffins, two each, and three large coffees. Silent, Ernie uncaps his and blows to cool it.

"You guys always hang around empty parking lots at six in the morning, naked?"

We concentrate on the food. John grins, closed and one-sided. Ernie stuffs his last bite in, wipes his fingers on the paper napkins. Gulps the rest of his coffee. Stands up. "Give me the key."

John fakes a hurt look, like a kid refusing spinach. "No."

I burst out laughing. But Ernie's serious. He waits, palm up.

"You have a key," John tells him.

"Damn right." Ernie strides out and in half a minute he's got his pants and shoes on and is heading to the car.

"Aren't you going to stop him?" I know exactly what he's going to do. John either doesn't know, or doesn't care anymore.

He wads up his sandwich paper and lobs it into the waste basket. Drinks his coffee.

I'm disappointed that Ernie drives off without me, but I cover it up by clearing away the rest of the trash. I want to turn on the tv but figure John's in no mood to see his wedding splashed all over the criminal news again.

"They said 'questioning' — so maybe if you go back and answer all their questions, you could stop running."

He studies me, as if he's tracing my actions since we met. "You finally believe I'm innocent."

"Yes." And Ernie, who at first was completely neutral, apparently has doubts or he wouldn't be orchestrating John's escape. Where along the way did we switch?

John gives me coins and I bring cartons of orange juice from the machines. It tastes pretty bad, but drinking it is something to do. After that, he goes outside to pace and smoke. I go to my room and put on the cut-offs and new shoes.

How to get rid of the old sneaks? The chance of anybody actually following us here and swabbing my DNA off them is zero, but I'd rather incinerate the evidence instead of leaving it in a waste basket.

"You watch too much tv," I mutter. Nobody's on our trail.

In an hour Ernie drives up in some strange car that he explains is a 'loaner.' He watches John's face, which tells me nothing. "Come on, old man, let's go for a drive."

"With you? In that? No thanks."

He doesn't ask what Ernie did with his Caddy. We both knew his intentions, and figure he's set them in motion. There's resignation in John's manner when he says, "You know how I felt about that car."

"She's in a safe place." Ernie leans from the waist like he wants to put his hand on John's shoulder. Instead, he props on his own kneecaps, his face in striking range, waiting for John to make a move.

A quick frown. John glances around the room, picks up the door key and sticks it in his pocket. "Let's ride, then."

In our hats and sunglasses, and a car like thousands of others, we should be able to go anywhere and do anything we want. I sense that Ernie has planned a surprise, so I just watch the passing scenery without comment.

It's more or less the same as what we came in on even though we're traveling in the same direction, until about twenty blocks later we hit a ritzy area of upscale stores and restaurants. Along side streets are huge old trees, landscaped lawns, and houses way grander than any I've seen except on tv or in magazines.

Soon we're passing a big lake, dotted with tiny tree-topped islands and bordered by a distant, wildlife-friendly other shore. Golf courses on the inland side, fancier restaurants, tiki bars, bait shops, and summer cottages. Docks and boats, and people in shorts and loud shirts swarming everywhere.

Ernie parks in a lot a few yards from the boat slips. Points. "That's ours." We follow him over gravel and packed sand and a weathered boardwalk to a cabin cruiser fit for a movie producer or lawyer.

Joking, I ask, "Does this boat go to the Cayman Islands?" He can afford to rent or even own such a thing. Then I remember that his trust fund is untouchable for two more months. Did he add his name on John's account at the bank? I can't see that happening. Not with John at his elbow.

"Just across the lake," he answers. When we're on board, he makes us put on life jackets, then adjusts knobs and reads gauges, shows us where the snacks are, and turns on a CD player. The New Age music suits me, though John rolls his eyes a bit. I help myself to a package of chocolate chip cookies and a bottle of spring water.

There's no fishing gear. There is a cell phone, and Ernie makes several calls that we can't hear because of the engine. The day is full of sunshine and wind, and even with choppy water that makes me hold on to the railing, I'm joyful and don't get seasick.

Twenty minutes later we've left the marina and most of the islands behind. Private landings, glimpses of mansions on the hillsides above. "How big is this lake?"

"Never measured it." He steers slightly to our right. One small island lies ahead. Woods come right down to the water's edge. As we move in closer, I watch the swell pound away at the bank, and realize the land is shaped like a loaf of bread, narrow, but maybe a mile long. At the far point, he navigates with caution to the only place suitable for a landing.

He cuts the engine and we sit in silence.

Slowly I become aware of song birds in the underbrush. A hawk sails overhead. John opens the fridge, turns away in disgust. We drift in close enough for Ernie to leap onto land and tie to an iron stake. "You guys coming?"

John eyes the lake and the wooded island. "I'm good here."

I get into position but the distance looks too risky. From a stable platform, yes; but the boat's not stable and the water churns against the bank. If I fall in, I won't drown but my running shoes will. "Jump," Ernie encourages, and I jump.

Grabbing at shrubs and kicking loose rocks and dirt, I scramble up to where he waits. The moment I'm on level ground, he takes off on a trail just wide enough for my feet, never mind the rest of me whipped by leafy limbs. The sunglasses darken everything but they protect my eyes.

I don't ask where we're headed. It's a secret, special place, and I'm glad John chose to stay behind. He can't leave in the boat as Ernie has the key.

This is more fun than the hikes Collins used to take us Middles on, across old pastures to the creek behind East Wind. Used to, since he stopped doing that the year Jerry nearly drowned Steve under the waterfall. Even after Jerry joined the Almost-Outs, Collins refused to hike anymore.

There are no waterfalls here, only boulders, moss, pines, old hardwoods that remind me of history lessons about the landings at Plymouth and Jamestown. I think of snakes and bears, but the way Ernie's plunging ahead, he's not worried. We must be close to the middle of the island when he slows to a halt. I look beyond him and at first see only more of the same.

Expecting the foundation of a burned cabin, at least, I finally spot a lump of brown canvas. A circle of melon-sized stones—a fire pit—clues me in. The brown lump is a one-man tent, fallen to wind, rain, and time. "Haven't been here for a while," he says. He steps to it almost on tiptoes. Hunkers and pulls at the rotten material.

Hunkering beside him, I barely hear the words, "I was too young to stay out here by myself." He pokes at the sodden lump with a stick. Snakes still on my mind, I scoot back, but nothing slithers out except a hairy-legged spider. He tosses the stick away and continues tiptoeing forward a few yards to a domed shelter built of saplings and covered with pine branches.

"This was going to be a sweat lodge." He gives a short unhappy laugh. "I sweated, all right, building it."

Brown needles still cling, though when he pulls at a limb, they shower an entrance so low he has to crawl inside. He reaches, draws me in with him. Too small for its purpose, the 'lodge' has plenty of ventilation because many of the poles have been displaced by the antics of squirrels or other animal. Crouched in the dim place, he finds the strength to admit, "Leaving is harder than I thought it would be."

Does he mean, leaving this for Canada? Or university? Does he even know. . . .

"It worked for John. I thought it would work for me, too, but it hasn't." He starts tearing the lodge apart from the inside, shoving off poles and branches until we're able to stand up, a circle of decaying wood surrounding us. He gazes at the forest, sniffing its aromas like a wild creature alert for danger. "I don't want to take this with me."

He kicks the pieces, destroying the shape, and I help him. I don't have the courage to probe into his reasons for returning to a place that made him miserable.

We find John asleep on one of the drop-down beds, an empty water bottle on the floor. "This'll wake him up," Ernie laughs. He starts the engine and revs it to a mellow roar. John swings his legs off the bed and sits up, groggy. "Is it lunch time yet?"

The clock surprises me. Ten forty-five. We were on the island for over an hour.

Zooming around the point, we head back the way we came. In about ten minutes we come to a shallow inlet. I'm surprised again when we travel along it for maybe a half a mile.

Ernie cuts the engine and expertly steers us into a covered boat slip. If it was noon, I'd think he was keeping a lunch appointment with well-to-do friends. Okay, eleven could mean brunch. With his tennis pals. Or his university roommate, come September.

I wish I had dressed better for this occasion, but at least my shoes aren't full of holes. John's in the pants and shirt from his father's dresser. No wonder Ernie calls him 'old man.' Too bad. In his jeans and black t-shirt, he could pass for an actor.

We walk up a winding, root-studded dirt path. Trees block a view of neighbors, if there are any. On a level space, a well-kept tennis court. Field houses made of stone. Steps leading up to a high brick wall. Next to a solid metal door, an entrance box accepts whatever code Ernie punches in.

When the door snaps shut behind us, I'm awed. John is too, judging by his silent inspection of a three-story brick house in a rich-and-famous setting. It's bigger than the East Wind library, nowhere near as old. Three-car garage, closed. Fresh-cut lawn, blooming shrubs, rustic benches under shade trees. Green and yellow aromas blend with cool shade and bright sun. And this is the servants' entrance.

"Your boat. Your home." I don't doubt it, but prod, to hear him say it.

"For now." He leads us past a side yard where three round tables are placed under a vine-covered wooden arbor, on a smooth brick patio that fills the space between the house and the high wall. Tables close enough for public conversations, far enough apart for private ones. Is this where Fran and Hoodoo hung out, before they ran away?

The front of the house is like the back, multiplied a few times. Beds of spring flowers on either side of a brick walkway. Benches under giant trees. No flamingos or gnomes, no tire swing, no dead lawnmower. Wide lawns slope to the brick wall and an iron gate with scrollwork that looks like grape leaves and clusters. A sidewalk on the other side, a street, but no houses to ruin the view.

Six brick columns rise from a porch. Two stone steps, a floor of some dark gray material that Ernie says is slate. Expensive-looking cushioned iron furniture—no plastic table and chairs to blow away in a summer storm. Double door with etched-glass panels and enough brass to make a tuba.

Inside, even though there's no marble, real or fake, I'm not disappointed. Two-story entry, central hallway, dining room to the left, entertainment center to the right. Dark stairs lead up to bedrooms; a long hallway to the right, to more bedrooms.

"Wait here," Ernie says, heading to the back, where there'll be a kitchen and a wing for the live-in staff. I'm okay with that. Waiting here gives me a chance to peek into the carpeted room outfitted with a theater-size movie screen, sound system, and shelves of tapes and DVDs. Sofas, tables with lamps, cabinets with who-knows-what behind locked doors.

The dining table seats a dozen, a silver service on a heavy lace tablecloth. China cabinets, buffets, a chandelier. An old-fashioned fireplace with gas logs, crystal candlesticks on the mantel, a huge mirror to reflect expensive dinners with friends, relatives, business partners.

It's what I've dreamed of, my incentive whenever school assignments got dull. I just thought I wanted to live in John's farmhouse.

Ernie emerges from the gloomy interior. "Everyone knows you're here, so make yourselves at home. Movie? Tennis? Early lunch on the terrace?"

"I want to see your room." The words leap from my mouth before I can consider the effect they'll have on him.

Or on John.

Episode 18

Ernie's hand rests lightly on the staircase railing. A glacial age passes before he says, "Go on up. You can't miss it." He adds, "I think John might prefer a fierce game of pool."

"You got that right." John grins. "I'll beat your— socks off."

Ernie leads him down to the game room, their footfalls almost silent on the carpeted steps. I touch the railing where Ernie's hand lay, and am puzzled by the dampness of a sweating palm. Anticipation to discover whatever he's nervous about makes me run up the two short flights connected by a landing.

I can't miss it because it takes up half the second story. Walls stretch away in a rectangle at my left to a row of open windows. Morning sun. Old-fashioned sheer curtains billow in little breezes.

At this end, across from the entry, is a bathroom. Usual stuff. One set of unused towels on the rack. On the counter, a few used toiletries meant for a male. After relieving myself, I return to those windows. The roofed terrace and tables seem far below, and leafy woods block my view of anything beyond the brick wall.

There's a leather swivel chair, worn to a comfortable shape and softness. Resting my head, I survey the desks and low bookcases on either side, book shelves and framed art and posters scattered above. Enough storage space for a dozen collections, starting with picture books and toy soldiers and moving through years of board games, school art projects and photo albums, videotapes and CDs and DVDs, novels and electronics, native artifacts and computer paraphernalia, textbooks and a telescope.

His bed is antique and huge, right next to the bathroom, and the matching six-drawer dresser is piled on top with small boxes and pottery. The only mirror is in the bathroom. The only clothes visible are jackets and caps on a coat tree. No stray socks under the bed, no dirties tossed in a corner. No old snack wrappers, not even in the trash basket. Is he this neat, or is there some paid maid? Mother is gone, so it's not her.

Shutting my eyes, I imagine him coming in from school. He tosses down his books, grabs a baseball and glove, rushes to play with friends. Sits at that desk, his study lamp angled just right, doing his homework. Writing term papers. Listening to music, reading for enjoyment.

I imagine him younger, nine maybe. Fran's only seven, pestering him to play dolls. He refuses. Later, when she's nine, she brings her book (what was the title? He told me. Dependable Fran) and being eleven, he flees, leaving her crying.

How would I have treated a younger sister? Probably the same. Girls in the foster homes were usually biting two-year-olds. I stayed out of their way. Older ones, but younger than me, carried around dolls not books, and were beneath my notice.

What I do notice is a framed photo among small trophies and a group of achievement medals pinned to a velvet-covered stand. Leaning close, I recognize Ernie beside a woman who must be his mom. They look alike, and happy. I don't see any pictures of his father or sister. Feeling sneaky, I skim through the top album.

The house, the school, school friends. Cub Scout troop. Boy Scouts. Youth group. Even teachers. Arty photos of objects arranged like still life paintings. Trees, squirrels, an occasional dog. The same dog, a mutt. He had a dog. Maybe.

But no dad. No Fran. There are blank spaces where things have been taken out.

I remember my camera and new film cartridge. Without a flash, the shots have to be made outside. I've skimmed the other two albums—more of the same—when I hear laughter downstairs, and then a single pair of footsteps coming up.

He's flushed and sweaty, the smile still on his face.

"Who won?"

"Who do you think?"

"You let the old guy win?"

"Of course. It's only polite."

He strips off shoes, pants, shirt—the same grungy outfit he's worn since the campground bathhouse—and heads into the shower. I realize what's been bothering me. Where's the sauna?

Jacuzzi? Oversize bath tub with rotating jets? Why doesn't he use the air conditioning? I know his class of people live that way. Which piece of Ernie's puzzle doesn't fit?

Picking up his clothes from the floor, I'm startled when a handful of cartridges fall out of the shirt pocket. I wonder when he unloaded Hoodoo's gun, and suspect it was long before I pulled the thing on John and said like a dork, "Blink."

I shove the bullets back into the pocket and glance around for something to be doing when he finishes. Not meddling in desk drawers. Not lounging on the bed, wrinkling the bedspread. Ah. A two-inch-thick school project notebook. Criminal Justice, pages and pages of neat notes with dates, and research papers based on case files. My heart flips a few times. Crazy thoughts bang around in my brain.

He's an undercover FBI agent, older than he looks, gathering evidence on John. Or, he's working for East Wind and any minute now O'Leary will walk in and slap cuffs on me. The house is really headquarters for a detective agency, not his home at all, and this room is his office. Then sanity returns. I once wrote a school project on string theory, go figure.

One of the cases is Frank Logan, AKA 'Hoodoo.' And I thought Jerry was a wacko.

Ernie comes out of the bathroom in a towel and raids the dresser for clean briefs, socks, and t-shirt. "You have time for a shower, if you want. Lunch won't be ready for another forty minutes."

While I'm making myself presentable, I can hear another shower on the other side of this wall and figure John's rousing game of pool has left him in a mellow mood. Not enough to sing, but relaxed enough to get naked in a strange rich man's home.

Ernie gives me a button-down-collar shirt from the back of his closet, and a pair of jeans somebody has ironed. He's comfortable in his preppy mode, loafers on his feet, wet hair slicked behind his ears. I wonder if John was willing to put on Ernie's father's clothes.

When we meet him at the glass patio doors, I see that he was. Knit shirt and pleat-front pants. We're a real trio, sauntering to the terrace for a meal served under the vine-roofed picnic area.

There's actually a maid arranging cloth napkins, silverware, pitchers of lemonade and iced tea, and dishes with silver dome covers. When she's out of earshot, Ernie says, "It's not what I wanted, but it's what they had."

John looks at the array of food, then at me. Now I understand why Ernie's nervous. John's voice in my mind's ear slams the coffee I'd made: 'Tastes like the stuff fancy places serve in a thimble.'

We chow down on the best stuff I've ever eaten in my life. Except for a mixed green salad, I don't know what half of it is, disguised in toppings and sauces, and the portions are small but satisfying. At least the dessert is recognizable. John and I both cry, "Junket!" And he adds, "Haven't had that in years. My mom used to make it every Friday night."

Ernie shrinks into an invisible shell, clearly dreading his guest's first taste.

Eyes on his dish, John admits, "This is better." And Ernie breathes again.

I haven't had this, ever. East Wind cooks don't make theirs from scratch, and I bet John's mom didn't either. It's strawberry, and I'm considering asking for seconds when the maid brings a fancy coffee pot and cups, along with a chocolate fudge cake with whipped cream, and something between the layers tastes like rum raisin ice cream. The coffee's strong, but mellow.

John cleans his plate without a word. Until the maid returns and says, "Chef would like to know what drinks you'll be wanting."

Drinks? I'm floating now. John holds his tongue until Ernie tells her, "I think lime margaritas would suit everyone," and she's gone inside. Then he spits out one: "Chef?!"

Ernie shrugs. "I don't sign his paycheck. Don't blame me.

A young man in a white shirt and black trousers brings another cart and clears the table. The maid returns and places cloth doilies, a larger one in the middle for the big pitcher. Sets frosted glasses, bowls on stems. Must hold at least a pint.

Lime is one of my favorite flavors, so the drink goes down way too fast. Though I'm already woozy, and hanging out with these two is bound to be bad for my liver, I fill the glass again. I wonder what Ernie's Criminal Justice instructor would have to say about giving alcohol to a minor. Funny, when the blonde was involved, he was mean to her, yet he's never objected to my drinking John's beer and he's okay with whatever is in a margarita.

Free, I think. Here, I'm free to do as I please. Under the vine-covered structure Ernie calls a pergola, it's quiet and shady. The angle of the sun arches over, and he says, "Anybody for tennis? Or will it be a nap?"

John seems to want to say a few things, but presses his lips together. I know he's thinking about the Caddy, not sure what to do about it. Or even what he wants to do about it. "Nap," he says. "Then you guys can entertain me with a tennis match. It ought to be worth watching."

We leave the dessert dishes, assorted glasses and cups, coffee pot and empty pitcher for the maid. At the bottom of the stairs, Ernie tells me, "I'll be down the hall there if you need me."

He walks the length of the corridor and enters a room at the end. Something tells me, it's his mom's room, and he wants to be alone.

Behind me, John leans close, says, "So what's your story?"

"What do you mean?"

"I know you two aren't brothers. He told me all about this Hoodoo character his sister ran off with, but not a damn word about you."

"I hitched a ride with them a few days ago, and kinda like life on the road." I try to stare him down, but when the corners of his mouth twitch in a losing battle with a grin, I look across the emerald lawn to the scrolly gate and think about Jerry's losing battle with the grass at East Wind.

John reads my mind. "I ran away once." He sobers. "Twice."

"Bet the first time was a lot more fun."

"Yeah." He taps a cigarette out of the pack. Thumbs open a matchbook. Pauses. "Vinnie, people this rich don't get that way honestly."

I'm stymied. To me, John's no longer poor, but there's a neat explanation for the source of his money. "I don't care. Ernie's not responsible for what his folks do."

I suspect that he feels he is. The Golden Boy. I bet he's got all twelve report cards in a drawer, straight A's. Awards, medals, probably newspaper articles. Big trust fund which caused all the anger. When Ernie's less nervous, when the three of us are toasting our toes on some beach, I'll dig the whole story out of him.

I spend the nap time lying on his bed, reading one of his books, *The Mills of God*, by William H. Armstrong. Mostly I'm outraged, and hope the ending justifies all this torture. It does.

When we assemble again, Ernie says, "Tennis will have to wait. She's ready." By 'she' he means the Caddy and I watch John for his reaction. His face is like a stone. Sunglasses and captain's hat in place, Ernie jingles the keys. "You guys coming?"

We return to the boat, cruise to the docks, drive the 'loaner' car to the Starshine to pick up our stuff. After the mansion experience, the seediness of the motel hits me in the face like a fist. Stale pizza and chocolate milk cartons in the trash can. Ratty carpet, streaked mirror, cardboard landscapes in plastic frames that remind me of the Morningbird. But I was happy here, for those few hours.

Ernie brings the extra rolls of toilet paper from the bathroom, and our eyes meet. "Free," I say, and he smiles. "Come on, Mouse, let's make John sweat."

"You really get a kick out of teasing him, don't you?"

He locks the motel room. "Stay with him while I turn in the key."

John's already sitting in the car. I open the door. "Where's your key." John tosses it to me, I yell "Hey!" and toss it to Ernie. "Every dollar counts."

143

Ernie drives us along a new route, so twisty I'm sure he's doing it to tantalize John. Saturday, not much work traffic but people running to and fro just the same. We pass through every kind of area from trendy shops to unbelievable shacks with small children playing in the yards.

Finally we arrive at what looks like a car dealership, body shop, storage building, parking garage complex. Ernie doesn't let the 'closed' signs on the doors stop him. He drives around to the back and cuts the motor. "Knock three times," he jokes, and we all get out.

He's not joking. A man in coveralls answers his coded summons by raising a metal door and letting us into a facility with at least ten bays. It's cleaner than I expected, though the smell of hot oil, fresh paint, and stuff I can't name fills the air.

John's eyes gleam at the sight of vintage and foreign cars on racks or lined up to be driven away. For the moment, he's distracted from the purpose of our trip. Then another man in a suit leaves an office, shakes Ernie's hand, says, "They're bringing her now."

When we see the Caddy roll into view, my spit dries up so I couldn't speak if I tried. Black, just like Ernie promised. The grill is different, too. He's watching John like an eagle zeroing in on a rabbit, and he's tensed to fight—or run.

John's stony face melts in anguish and I expect a heart-rending wailing to rip from his throat as he grabs Ernie and cracks his head against the concrete floor before any of the men here can stop him.

He's trembling all over, his gaze riveted on the Caddy coming slowly towards us.

144

Episode 19

The driver turns the car slightly, so we're not seeing it head-on. Stops. Like some fashion model, angling to show off her dress. I wish I'd brought my camera, but I left it on the hall table after we'd all snapped shots of each other after lunch.

John explodes—into laughter. A quick startled look at him, then I see the Caddy in all its glory ten feet away. It's not the same car. Ernie laughs, too, but his glee is cut short. John lunges for him, and Ernie takes off running.

The driver gets out and Ernie jumps in. He locks the doors and John beats on the window, then slaps the hood. "You better hide, you little shit. I'll get you for this."

Men standing around don't seem to know whether to cheer or haul John away. I break the tension. "So where's the pink one?"

Head honcho answers without taking his eyes off John, who's by now kicking the tires and threatening to rip off the driver's door. He and Ernie are still laughing. "It's in a safe place."

"That's what Ernie said."

"Who?"

His question confuses me, but I don't follow up since in spite of John pounding on the windshield, Ernie's creeping the car toward the open bay. He brakes and unlocks the doors long enough for me to dive into the back seat. John moves to block our path. Ernie honks the horn, cranks down the window, yells, "Get in old man!"

When we're on the road again, there's total silence except for air whooshing through the open windows. The route back is more direct, a four-lane through a busy part of town, then past a big hospital, a park, and a school.

We enter a gated community not much different from East Wind except that these are inhabitants, not inmates, and can leave whenever they want.

Three blocks later we're at Ernie's front gate. While the electronics open it, Ernie says, "I couldn't resist."

"Joker. Just you wait."

We drive through, and Ernie stops his Caddy on the brick parking area outside the glass patio doors. Above, his old-fashioned curtains flutter like white banners.

"So, where is she?" There's no anger in John's voice. There is an edge.

"Locked in one of their storage units." Ernie gives him a key attached to a small plastic disc with a number on it. "Until you need her."

John ponders it. "How does a kid like you learn how to do so much?"

Ernie goes around, opens John's door. "Necessity."

The missing puzzle piece. I'm positive it has to do with the determination to earn his dad's approval. Maybe his gold has always been tarnished, and Francine was the final straw, beyond fixing. He will go with us, at least until the fall, when classes begin.

On the way into the house, John says, mildly, "I guess finding a Caddy like this in a few days by phone is easy for a rich boy wanting to pull a prank."

"Didn't buy her just to fool you," Ernie tells him. "Two years ago, I rescued her out of a cornfield. Having money helped with the restoration though."

John looks at him with fresh respect. "You do have good taste."

"Thanks." He turns to me. "So, want to work up an appetite?"

"Tennis? Sure." I hated tennis as a PE class, but this might be my only chance to play on a private court. He takes the stairs two at a time and clatters down with a couple of racquets and a can under his arm. He should be in whites, but he's not. A headband corrals his hair, and he shoves another onto my head. Over my eyes. I adjust it, following him along the hallway and down to the fence.

I pick one of the racquets. John picks a shady bench and lights up a fresh cigarette.

I know I can't win against Ernie, but give it my best shot. We race about, letting off steam, entertaining ourselves as well as John, who laughs at our antics, and I'm hungry long before dinner is to be served in the dining room. He doesn't throw the game, and I'm grateful. I take more pictures of us down at the courts.

"Dinner and a movie," John muses, his thoughts far away in his past.

"Yeah, pick one while the kid and I clean up."

He lets me go first, while he makes some calls on the cell phone he's brought from the boat, and afterward I try on knee shorts and another crisp shirt from his closet. This could become a habit. When he's done with his second shower of the day, I have to ask, "How come you don't use the air conditioning?"

"Irresponsible use of refrigerants will be the death of the planet. Besides, I don't like being cold either."

"Then we better steer John away from Canada."

"I've just been doing that."

"What do you mean?"

"My dad's on the case. He's pretty sure he can clear John of any charges."

Panic rises from the pit of my stomach. "And your dad is—who?"

"You've never heard of him, but he's got pull. Thomas Gordon, Atty."

Seconds pass before I can think straight and remember that 'Atty' is short for 'attorney.' I've seen it written, but never heard anyone say it. Never expect to again. So it wasn't a fancy lunch that had him sweating. It was the prospect of calling on his father for help. "You told him everything?"

"Not everything. I put him on Jordan's trail, and it's leading straight to a murder conviction." He combs his hair and then takes a whack at mine. "Don't mention it, it's not a done deal yet."

This warning sticks with me through a dinner fit for a shark lawyer's son and his friends. John comments, "Now this is a

147

man's meal." He digs into the steak. Gravy, dinner rolls, vegetables, and a red wine that Ernie withholds from me, saying, "You know what happened last time, Mouse."

"Yeah, after half a bottle," I counter. Settle for spring water, with the promise of coffee with dessert.

Dessert is coconut cake. I swear I see tears in John's eyes when the maid sets his slice in front of him. I take a bite of mine and understand what 'bliss' means. Freshly grated coconut, layers juicy with real coconut milk, foamy white icing.

A dim memory struggles out of the past. A hammer striking something hollow. Peeled pieces in my hand, crunching under five-year-old teeth. There's a trimmed tree, lights blinking. I almost see my mother's face, then it's gone.

"My mom used to make cakes like this," John says. I don't say anything.

"Save room for popcorn with the movie," Ernie tells us.

Too late.

At least, I think that until we head for the entertainment center. A familiar aroma wafts through the door when a server opens it. His cart is stocked with carbonated drinks. There's an actual theater popcorn machine, and the hot cardboard box in my hand reminds me of Saturday afternoons spent in the Hackett cinema. When I became a Middle, no dorm master was willing to field trip us anymore, so it's been awhile.

John's choice is *Talladega Nights*. Ernie wants *Dead Poets Society*. He shows me *Chariots of Fire*, and I'm impressed that he knows me so well. We watch them in order (John sleeps through Ernie's), and six hours later we stagger out, bleary and stuffed with food and film. Ready for sleep, a late wake-up call, breakfast under the pergola.

Alone in Ernie's room, I try to recapture my mom's face, her voice, her laughter. But all I'm left with is the taste of sugary coconut cake and salty tears. Even so, I decide this is the best night of my life. John's case is as good as won, Ernie's on better terms with his dad, and the promise of escaping with friends to a new life of adventure fuels my imagination.

For a long while I toss and turn, planning how to disguise my appearance and what I'll do about school, and imagining where we'll all end up living.

But I've fallen asleep because something jars me awake.

Tense, I listen to silence. Was I dreaming? If I was, the dream wasn't pleasant and the sound I think I heard scares me. It was the ring of a tire iron on bricks.

Rolling off the bed, I run to the open windows and look out. The security light shows me the black Caddy, and damned if the hood isn't raised. I open my mouth to call something rude to Ernie, but the person tinkering with the car must sense he's been spotted and straightens up. Hoodoo!

Drawing back so he doesn't see me, I figure by the time I alert John or Ernie, he'll finish whatever he's doing and be out of the neighborhood. His gun is still in the bed roll, there on Ernie's big leather chair, and the cartridges are still in Ernie's shirt pocket, there on the floor.

I pull on Ernie's knee shorts and fill the magazine. My hands are shaking but I've seen this stuff in movies and a loaded gun puts me in charge. Creep down the stairs. Open the glass door and step onto the bricks.

He's easing the hood shut so it doesn't make any noise, and can't see me in the shadow of the patio roof. "Hold it right there, Hoodoo."

Startled, he races to the picnic area and starts climbing the pergola, toward the top of the brick wall.

I don't intend to let him invade Ernie's home and get away with it, so I run forward, aiming for his legs and praying to hit one of them. I squeeze the trigger. The world explodes. Something smacks my face hard near one eye, something else delivers a stunning blow to the back of my head.

Did Hoodoo have another gun? If I'm shot through and through, there must be an afterlife because I'm still conscious. Numb and dizzy. A tingling in my hands warns me moments before shocking pain shoots through them. The eye is wet with what must be blood and I'm afraid to open it, the other shows me Hoodoo scrambling over the vine-covered woodwork.

Another shot, behind me. Hoodoo screeches and grabs his leg and rolls off the roof. John's on him like a tv cop, holding him down, shouting for help. Then Ernie's pressing a wadded cloth against my head and yelling, "Call 911! Call the police!"

"I'm okay." But I don't think he hears me, because people come out of the house, and a middle-aged man ties Hoodoo's hands and ankles with a piece of electrical wire. The maid's on a cell phone, trying to make the 911 operator listen instead of asking stupid questions.

John's kneeling beside us. He says, "Where are the keys?" Ernie says, "On my dresser." John orders, "Get him in the car."

Ernie doesn't argue. He scoops me off the ground, and the man who tied up Hoodoo opens the door for him. John's in almost as soon as we are, and we're backing down the driveway toward the front gate. Ernie holds me on his lap, pressing the cloth so hard against my head I'm afraid my brain is showing. My head doesn't hurt yet, there's a truckload of cotton between my ears.

We race through the winding blocks of dark silent homes, flashes of street lights like strobes in my good eye. I close it, and can hear faraway sirens through the cotton. "Cops or ambulance?" John doesn't have to stop at the community gate, it's already open for emergency vehicles, whenever they arrive. Ernie answers, "Both."

We pick up speed. A lot of speed. John says, "We'll be at the hospital while they're still looking at house numbers."

Flashing lights pass us, two sets, screaming toward Ernie's house. I'd like to be there, to see if the cops and EMS fight over who takes Hoodoo. The big efficient looking hospital buildings are maybe a dozen or fifteen blocks away, and figure I'll probably live to tell this tale after all. Until the whole car starts to shake and there's a clatter of metal on metal. John mutters, "Uh-oh."

What has Hoodoo done? I forgot to tell them he was messing under the hood.

I don't have time to say anything before there's a giant WHUMP and I hope we haven't hit a dog, or worse, a person crossing the four-lane on foot. "Oh God!" John cries as the Caddy takes a screeching nosedive and the rear end rises into the air. "Hold on—!"

"What hap—" Ernie begins, but we're in a full somersault and he's shielding my head with his arms when we fly off the back seat and crash against the dashboard. Slow motion, just like I've always read about.

But we were going at least eighty, so when the Caddy smashes upside down on the tarmac, the doors spring open. Without seat belts, we're all thrown onto the grassy median.

It's strangely quiet. The sirens fade into the distance. Then one of them makes a U-turn and screams back on our side of the highway. I want it to be the EMS, rescuing us, but it isn't. Badges and guns flash in the headlights and an authoritative voice strides toward us. "What the hell? Is anybody hurt?"

John's alive because he answers, "The kid's been shot. Get him to the hospital."

There's another unfamiliar voice, closer to me. "This one isn't moving."

I wave my bleeding left hand but I'm on the dark side of the car, and suddenly whether he sees me doesn't matter. A huge pain in my chest and shoulder blots out all thoughts except the fear that my back is broken.

"He's breathing," the first badge says, and I hear them slapping someone's face and asking stupid questions. It isn't my face, so they probably think Ernie's the one shot. It's a relief to know my companions aren't dead. Before I can make the officers aware of me, all the lights go out.

Episode 20

It's Christmas and our living room is warm and softly lit. Holiday music plays on a radio. The tree sparkles with blinking lights and tinsel. Tinsel's my favorite, and I'm given a handful with the caution to get it all on the tree. She pops a peppermint cane into my mouth.

I put the strands on one by one instead of tossing them in clumps, so the pleasure of trimming the tree will last. Peppermint juice escapes onto my chin, but I can't take the cane out because handling it will make the filmy tinsel stick to my fingers. She's my mom and I want to please her.

Blinking lights zoom off the tree and swirl around me, mostly an angry red, not Rudolph or Santa or the stripe on a candy cane. The radio music turns ugly, like the winding down of a siren.

The wreck. Ernie. John. The Caddy. The bag of money, the sweat lodge, lunch on the terrace, running for an out-of-bounds tennis ball, shooting at Hoodoo.

There's a rush of cold air and I think it's my dad opening the front door, carrying last-minute gifts for us. Then there's a lot of urgent conversation and rushing footsteps, pain in my head and hands, I'm in my narrow bed and it's flying through the night.

When I crawl out of the dark pit again, the room is light, not bright. I'm lying on my back, and the pain is muffled. Ears still feel stuffed with cotton. Bandage over my eye. Not on my eye, thank God.

Venturing to open both, I see Ernie asleep. His chair is pulled close enough that he's slumped on my bed. They've shaved a place for the sterile pad taped to the back of his head, though uncut hair mostly covers it. His left wrist is wrapped.

My hands are covered with soft white gloves, like a burn victim. A brace on my left shoulder. What did I break? Shoulder blade? Rib? Collar bone? At this point, I'm just glad we're in a place where we're being taken care of.

"John?" I'm unsure if he's around the corner, or even in the hospital.

Ernie's not asleep, because he sits up as soon as he hears me speak. He looks like he's about to cry and my heart flip-flops. Is John dead? In jail? Is Ernie upset over the wreck of the black Caddy? Have the Suits finally found me?

"I'm so sorry," he says, and that tells me nothing.

"You're always sorry," I say stupidly. "Mostly without reason."

"I should have thrown away those damn cartridges. Should have warned you that gun was a dangerous piece of shit, just like Hoodoo."

"What happened to him?"

"Arrested for all sorts of things, mostly kidnapping Francine." He smiles.

"Is she okay?"

"He dumped her on a street corner in Taylorsville. Once she got to a shelter and called Dad, yeah, she's fine."

In the hallway people clatter stuff on carts, call to each other, give bursts of laughter. In the next room a tv blares the jangley music of a game show.

"He is crazy."

"Unfortunately that's probably true so the bastard will likely end up in a psycho ward instead of where he belongs."

I start to draw a deep breath, but the medication has worn off. "What'd I break?"

"Collarbone. Pinky on your right hand."

"What's wrong with my head?" I try to raise my eyebrows, which doesn't work too well because of the bandage.

"Not as bad as it looked last night," he tells me. "Part of the pistol gave you a nasty gash that bled a t-shirt full and then some."

All over your car seat, I think, before realizing the car is probably totaled. "It's all my fault for not waking you when I saw him in the yard."

153

Before either of us can move on to another topic, like where's John or what's going to happen now, a slender middle aged woman appears in the doorway. I recognize her from the framed photo in Ernie's room. She's pretty, shoulder-length light brown hair, and wearing a pink-flowered summer dress and sandals. A shoulder bag matches them, but nothing about her shouts 'money.'

He turns to follow my look, half rises, gasps, "Mom."

She doesn't seem to know what to say, or do. Neither does he. They start toward each other, stop, then a few steps more and they're hugging. I figure they'll go into the hall or to a waiting room, but no, they're coming toward me.

"Mom, this is Vinnie—"

He's never heard my last name. I've always suspected the East Wind records were made up by some joker who thought I should answer to Vinnie. Vinnie the Weenie.

To ease Ernie's embarrassment, I bite the bullet and introduce myself. "Hello, Mrs. Gordon, I'm Vincent Scott."

Her smile is shaky, like she doesn't know what to say to me either. My bruises and bandages must look worse than I thought, and she's careful not to offer to shake my injured hand. He seats her in the only chair, a plastic oversize thing that makes her seem younger and more uncertain than ever. "Your dad called. A candy striper told me where to find you."

"So you know Franny's home?"

"Yes. And that awful boy is in jail. I hope she'll testify against him."

"Dad will see to it that she does."

"What about you, Tommy? The doctor said you have a concussion. Shouldn't you be in bed?"

Hearing her call him Tommy throws me, then I remember how confused I was when the man at the body shop didn't know who I meant by 'Ernie.' Seems we're all sailing along under assumed names, one way or another.

"We both have a light concussion, but we're fine, really. Be out tomorrow."

154

And then—what? I don't have to wonder long, because a large man strides into my room and declares, "Vincent, I see you're on the mend. We'll send a car when you're done with the hearing, and you'll be home in no time."

It's O'Leary. My tongue sticks to the roof of my mouth so tight I can't even ask for a drink of water. He takes my silence as gratitude or something, and turns to Mrs. Gordon. She looks startled.

O'Leary doesn't notice, he talks about the weather, how happy he is that nobody was hurt (?!?) in the wreck, and how East Wind security has been beefed up so nothing like this will ever happen again. His parting shot at me is, "Don't worry, you won't have to testify at the trial. It's just a hearing and I know you'll tell the truth. You're a good boy."

He says to the others, "Straight A's, don't know what got into him." Then he's gone.

We all let out a huge sigh, and then laugh. Ernie's mom is a warm, sweet person, when her tense face relaxes. Even in a situation like this, it's not permanently lined by anger, the way my foster mothers' faces were.

Ernie briefly explains how we met at the picnic grounds and have been traveling together, but he leaves out specifics, like where I came from, or how we hooked up with John. She doesn't show much interest anyway. She's more concerned about Ernie's part in what's coming next.

"There'll be two hearings," he explains. "One for Hoo— Frank, and one for John." To me, he adds, "You'll testify only at John's, and it's set for day after tomorrow."

So John's alive and able to face whatever goes on at a hearing. He'd better be. I decide to rely on my innocent look and scholastic track record, and play dumb.

Ernie's mom opens her shoulder bag. I expect her to offer him cash, but it's a credit card. She avoids chewing him out for letting Fran or Hoodoo steal the other one. "You have your cell?"

"Yes."

"Everything you need?"

"Yes, Mom. Everything's okay. We'll be in touch."

"See that you are." She leans and hugs him again, holding him a long while. At the door she turns. "You know where to find me."

He lifts his chin once to mean 'yes,' and she's gone. "I like her," I say, and he says, "Me, too."

We're silent for several long minutes. The hall noise hasn't stopped, the tv has. I mention that I'm starving.

"Well, you missed breakfast, and judging by the menu they brought around, you won't be thrilled with lunch."

"Smuggle me in a cheeseburger."

"If I could, I would, for both of us."

Another dead spot. I'm sweating over O'Leary showing up, nervous about the hearing. Ernie pours ice water into a glass and bends the straw so I can drink. "You talked to your dad today?"

"Last night. He flew in from that conference this morning. Grace has been gathering evidence and once he's digested all the facts, he'll build a case against Jordan."

"What if John lied?"

"When everything's laid on the table, we'll know."

I don't plan to lay everything on the table. "What about the money? The fake ID. And those strings you pulled."

"What money?" Ernie grins, and I have my cue.

We eat lunch together in my room. Soggy veggies, tough mystery meat, and school Jell-O. Unlike other East Winders, I've never thrown mine against a wall to see if it sticks or bounces, especially when it's lime. The taste reminds me of the margarita.

Between bites, and gulps of milk, he fills me in on John. "Fractured his ankle, broke a rib, and cried like a baby when he saw the Caddy smashed like a drink can."

"You didn't cry?"

"Nah. I know where there's another one. Mint condition, like she's right off the factory floor."

"Pink?"

We grin. "So where is he now?"

156

Ernie sobers. "In custody. Bond is set at fifty thousand, but I can't pay it with my own money and I'm not going to involve Mom."

I wonder if John's thinking of Margie, the farmhouse, shooting Jordan, shooting Hoodoo. Frank. If Ernie's dad is the lawyer he's supposed to be, all of John's actions have been justified. Except not coming forward when the story broke.

'Hell,' I can hear him say, 'I was off fishing and didn't know anybody wanted me.'

That's what one of the Suits brought up that day in the coffee shop, so the idea's not that far-fetched. And since we did fish, we all should be able to use the alibi with a ring of truth behind it.

Ernie says, "Want me to read to you?"

"Sure." Then a nurse comes in and adjusts the drip and I don't hear past the first paragraph of some story in a magazine he's brought with him.

My dreams are not all sweet but when I wake around supper time, I can't remember any of them, and Ernie's gone. He's left the magazine, and a note: Mouse, I'm in Room 328. Send someone if you need me.

A child protection agency person arrives and stays with me until I'm discharged into her care. I'm not allowed to talk to anyone connected with the hearing, and don't have access to a phone. It's like being in a strange foster home again for two endless nights, and then I'm on stage alone without a copy of the script or any clue which character I'm supposed to be.

At the hearing, I tell the truth, nothing but the truth. The whole truth is none of the judge's business.

So I leave out the part about Jerry and Steve's plan to escape our prison, the fact that Jerry gave me money, and their help in getting over the wall. I definitely leave out everything about Al, and John's two-o'clock-in-the-morning wailing that scared the pee out of me. Well, it could have been a ghost for all I know.

The judge is gray-haired, overweight, and a poker player. Harder to read than Ernie or even John. What will he buy?

157

"After seeing that woman's body pulled up out of that well, I must've had a kind of breakdown. Felt like I had to get away from the place. I had bus fare from savings. East Winders always get charitable gifts at Christmas. I traded off toys I didn't want, for money." In Boy Scout mode again, I'm encouraged when he nods, like he understands.

He reveals that he already knows I met Hoodoo, Francine, and Ernie in the picnic area, and since the gun is what got me into this present mess, I explain how we came to have it, ending with, "Ernie was trying to keep Hoodoo—Frank—from killing anybody."

What else can I say? I wait for him to ask a question, he just nods a 'go-on.'

I don't mention the blonde in the red convertible, and since Ernie had warned me that breaking and entering is a felony, I skip over our night at Haw Creek Elementary School. Instead, I concentrate on our adventures at the thrift store, the rest areas, the cafes, and the coffee shop in the town where we saw—I almost call them 'Suits' but catch myself—Martin and the reporter.

I admit that's where we met John. Keeping the pink Caddy under wraps, I talk about the festival and what a great time we all had. Not wanting to paint too sweet a picture, I think twice before going into some detail about our stay at the farmhouse.

"So you were never held hostage by this—" He checks the papers on the table in front of him. "John Burand?"

"No, sir. We were out of money and needed a ride. He wanted somebody to help with the camp tent."

"And did he tell you why he was camping?"

"We fished in a stream where he used to go with his dad."

The judge gazes over his half-glasses at me for a long time. "And then Thomas Gordon—known to you as Ernie—invited both you and Mister Burand into his home."

Feeling near the end of the inquisition, I breathe deep, try to relax. "Yes, sir."

"Because Thomas Gordon's father is an attorney, and Mister Burand believed legal counsel to be necessary."

"I guess so." I'm still trying to get used to hearing Ernie's real name.

"So, to your knowledge, there was no connection between the murdered woman and Mister Burand."

Lying on small matters is easy. Lying outright to a direct question by a man who probably knows the answer chokes me. "I knew she was his wife."

"He never told you about their problems, or why she left him?"

"No, sir." No, he told Ernie.

"And after Mister Burand shot and wounded Jordan, you weren't frightened to be in his company?"

"That was self-defense."

"Were you there?"

"No, but our camp was five minutes away by foot and we heard the guns firing just the way John explained it."

"So when you shot at Frank Logan at the Gordon residence, you believed he had done something to the car."

"He had. He loosened the wheel so it would come off and maybe kill somebody."

The judge sits back, twiddles his pen with three fingers, watches me. I try to pull a poker face, too, though with only a giant gauze patch instead of the bulky bandage, my eyebrows have a life of their own. They rise in a silent question. Are we done here?

"That's all. Thank you." He leans forward and writes on his legal pad.

Slowly I stand up. "Sir. Will I be sent back to East Wind?"

His eyelids flick up at me, his hand pauses over the notes. "I'm afraid so."

He sounds genuinely sorry. I swallow my disappointment.

Episode 21

When the East Wind driver comes for me, I'm more than glad to go. My duffel bag is still at Ernie's house, along with my shoes and camera, so besides the t-shirt, briefs, and knee shorts I had on the night of the wreck, handed to me in a plastic hospital bag, all I leave with are the two-day-old charity items I'm wearing, courtesy of the foster family whose name I've already forgotten.

The driver's a middle-aged man I've never seen and we say absolutely nothing for the 200 miles to the school. I make a note to myself to ask for a map and push pin the places I've been, if I can find them. During the trip, my mind races in circles, with pit stops in between.

Did John's hearing go as planned? Has Ernie's dad built a case against Jordan, enough to bring him to trial and put him away for killing Margie?

Hoodoo's leg must be healing faster than my collarbone. Where is Ernie's mom now? Fran's probably already in some rehab place for wayward girls. Mostly I'm sorry I didn't have a chance to say a few last words to Ernie. Tommy. Tommy Gordon, son of Thomas Gordon, Atty.

I toy with the idea of legally changing my name to Scott Vincent. I never liked 'Vinnie' and am more uncomfortable with it than ever. Mouse suited me better.

We arrive just before supper time and nothing seems different, except the trees are in full leaf and the grass has been cut. The driver sets me off at my dorm. On the way in, I toss the hospital bag into a trash can.

O'Leary meets me in the lobby. Waiting for me, like a spider. "Vincent, I trust this escapade has made a proper impression on you. You'll find Mister Gregory more vigilant than your former dorm master, so henceforth I want only good reports. Agreed?"

"Yes, sir," I answer, suspicious at the emptiness of the lobby and the corridor beyond. The poison he injected fails to paralyze me.

Passing the dorm master's office, I see new Gregory working at old Collie's desk. He's a younger version of O'Leary. Doors on my hall are open, but everyone's either at supper or in town for some recreation. The third week in June is deceptively daylight, so I could be off about the time.

My room seems stifling, small. A few of Steve's things are on my side, but he's not here. What will everyone think when I appear in the mess hall? Have they been warned about my injuries? Will I be an outcast, or a secret hero? I really don't care. I lie down on my cot and try to relax. Impossible with the sling on my arm, so I take that off, but a lack of medication is starting to catch up with me.

Footsteps in the hallway. I sit up. From the quick shift in Steve's face, he's been briefed. A bit of a shock when he sees the deep bruises on mine, the sling on the floor beside my bed, the plastic shield on my right hand to protect the broken finger. "Hey," he says.

"Hey," I say.

He flops down in the only comfortable chair, placed between our sides of the room and meant to be shared. "You didn't tell."

"Did you think I would?"

"Hoped you wouldn't. Jerry's in D-hall right now for throwing old Collie's teeth in the john, but he'll be out tonight. Collie's gone. On sabbatical, they told us."

"So how long has the new guy been in charge?"

"Long enough to lay down the law."

I've been AWOL for only 13 days, so he must be quick on the trigger. "Where is everybody?"

"Doing laps. He says we're out of shape. But all it does is give me an appetite." Steve leans forward, elbows on his knees. "Is it true? What we heard on tv?"

"What did you hear?"

"That you were in a wreck that totaled an antique car that belonged to a murderer. And it was his wife we saw dragged out of the old well."

"Who the hell put that on the news?"

Steve looks startled at my language and sharp tone. "Some reporter named Bob Something. Said he'd been following the case for days."

"Yeah, I guess he was. But his story's crap." We stare at each other, him waiting for me to set things straight, me challenging him to ask another stupid question.

He gives up first, and comes over to high-five me. "Good to have you back, Mouse." I return the gesture, but then he eyes me and adds, "I guess it's you."

If it's not, it soon will be. Jerry comes in, does a little victory dance that reminds me of Hoodoo, and yells, "Vinnie, my man! How's the collarbone?"

"Hurts," I tell him. He offers me a half dozen pink and blue pills bound up in plastic wrap. I'm glad when the dinner buzzer sounds and everybody rushes out, since that keeps him from asking what I did with his money.

The Jell-O is red and rubbery. Jerry flings his at Eric. It bounces off Eric's head into the aisle, and Gregory hauls Jerry out of his chair by the ear and orders him to stand in the corner. Shoves Jerry's plate in his hand, and I think, Oboy! a huge fight is coming. I get ready to duck and cover.

They stand toe to toe for what feels like a minute but can't be more than half, before Jerry mutters "Sorry" and carries his plate to a table near the kitchen doorway. Standing because there's no chair, he finishes his meal. We finish, too, cowed. I was wrong. Things HAVE changed.

When Steve and I are in our room, he explains how Gregory got the upper hand so completely. "Oh they had it out the first day. Gregory beat the snot out of him."

"Bet that one's off the books."

"O'Leary doesn't know. He's in his own little world, delirious to have Jerry under control and you safe and almost sound."

After their first curiosity over the sling, deep bruises, and the patch on my head, the guys on our hall forget about me. I pick up my half-finished library book and block out the noisy board games and horseplay happening in other rooms, and Steve playing his clarinet.

Past curfew, I sneak to the pay phone. If there's news I want to hear it straight. The only listing in the directory is under Thomas Gordon, but I dial it anyway, hoping a maid will take the call and put Ernie on the line. An answering machine in his dad's office picks up, so I don't leave a message.

Normally I would never trust any pill Jerry could get his hands on, but if these few hours at East Wind are a sample of what's to come, I'm going to need something to dull my senses. The hospital doctor predicted that concussion cotton disappears in a week or two, and the collarbone should knit without complication in six weeks. The pinky should heal faster.

Passing a fountain, I take one of the pills. This time, I'm careful not to let the water wash it out of my mouth and down the drain.

I miss Ernie. John. Sailing down unfamiliar highways in a Caddy. Steve's clock dial glows in the darkness. After two a.m. He's snoring and I can't sleep. The pill has eased my pain and I don't notice the cotton so much when I'm not talking. Thank God it's summertime and there's no homework due tomorrow.

After breakfast, when I've been here more than a week and am dying of boredom, Gregory singles me out. "Vinnie, the counselor is ready to see you in his office. Nine, sharp. Don't be late."

Mister Jarvis has been at East Wind forever. I remember being counseled by him each time I was returned from a foster home. He's a nice old codger but he makes me nervous just the same. Today I notice his hair's really gray. Wrinkles. Brown spots on his hands. Getting stooped, too.

He motions me to the interrogation chair sized for Middles, and freshens a pencil on an old-fashioned sharpener bolted to the window frame. I know it's only for show, because he records sessions in pen. He sits down, opens a folder.

"Well, Vinnie." He always starts this way, with a long pause afterward. Then, "Do you want to tell me anything?"

"Not really."

"You're settling in okay?"

"Sure." It's not like I've been gone for months, like when I was being farmed out for a taste of family life.

"Well. I have some things to tell you."

I sit up straighter. New rules? News of John? Someone wants to adopt me at this late date? That's a laugh. But my palms sweat while I'm waiting for him to find words.

He clears his throat. Applies so much pressure to the pencil he's fiddling with that it breaks in half. He throws the pieces into his trash can. "I'm retiring at the end of the month."

This doesn't seem to require my input, so I just nod.

"I remember when you came to us. If I'd been married, I would have adopted you myself. You've been an exemplary student."

Until now, I hear his thought continue.

"And if I were married, I'd still give it some thought."

I'm thankful he's never married. I can't imagine living with him. Into a long silence, one question pushes at my lips and finally escapes. "If I was so adoptable, why didn't anyone else want me?"

He gives me a sad look, and I just know he's never going to answer that. But he does.

"Your birth mother wanted to keep you safe here. We sent you to homes only to comply with state regulations."

I croak words that are statements, not questions. "You know her. Who she is. Where she is."

He gives me that look again. "Yes."

I can't say anything. Can't think.

"You'll be free to find her, when you're of age."

I knew that already. Five years more?

"She has never forgotten you, nor given up her intention of revealing herself when she can."

I didn't know that. "Why can't she?"

"It's complicated."

The old fart thinks he's being kind, but I'm filled with rage. Maybe he's only soothing his conscience for keeping quiet. He doesn't mention my father, and that's a bad sign.

My mind clicks back to that radio news broadcast I heard in the farmhouse. The newsbit ended with ". . . an anonymous tip." I remember thinking Collins would have kept quiet when he did bed check and found me gone. He might have said something to the old counselor, hoping for help in searching, but Jarvis would have gone straight to O'Leary. The leak was out, Collins was fired, and Reporter was on my trail.

I stand up. My fists clench and it takes all my strength to keep from hitting him. "Happy retirement." I walk out.

Complicated. What does that mean? She's married again? Ill and unable to take care of a kid who's almost a teenager? Too poor to send me to a good school, so I'm a ward of the state most of my life?

I wish I'd never known freedom and adventure. Wish I'd stayed here and spent the summer in the pool or on the basketball court, whenever I wasn't in the library. Maybe without all the uproar and drama, Jarvis would have simply toddled off to his new life without feeling the need to ruin mine.

I'm in the bathroom between our room and the next, about to swallow the rest of Jerry's pills, when someone in the hall yells, "Vinnie! Telephone!"

When I reach the lobby, a tv newscaster is interviewing John on the steps of a court house with a tall man who must be Atty Gordon. Grabbing up the dangling phone, I shout, "Hello?"

"Vinnie, I got your message."

"You couldn't have. I didn't leave one." Ernie's voice is as much a relief as seeing John in an ankle brace instead of chains.

"We have caller ID. I would have gotten back to you sooner, but I was out of town gathering evidence. Is everything okay?"

"Better than okay. Are you watching tv? I just saw John and I guess it's your dad, leaving a court house with big smiles. Does this mean he's been cleared?"

"Pretty much. Jordan's in jail, and Dad has a copy of his signed confession."

"Wow! That was quick."

"His secretary and I did all the paperwork. The rest was just fanfare."

There's a silence, everything else I wanted to say has flown out of my head. Our connection is so clear he sounds like he's in the next room. Wish he was.

"Vinnie, I have a surprise for you. It ought to be there next week. In time for July Fourth."

"What is it?"

"It'll be nice."

"What color is it? Is it bigger than a bread box?"

"All colors, and I won't answer the last question. You'll just have to see it."

"How's your mom?"

"Oh, she's calmed down. Never better."

I want to ask more but he signs off with, "Behave and stay out of D-hall."

All colors, hmm. Must be prints of the pictures we took. He's had the film developed and is mailing the photos to me. Maybe my camera, too.

"Damn! Wish I'd told him to send me my running shoes." Then I remember it's Ernie, and he probably thought of that himself.

Glad I didn't take those pills, I go to my room whistling the last tune Steve played on his clarinet. Ernie hasn't abandoned me. Whatever the surprise is, it will be here for our East Wind Fourth of July celebration.

Episode 22

During a baseball game which our dorm Middles are losing, Jerry sidles up to me on the bleachers and says, "Okay, Mouse, where's the money?"

We don't see Jerry much anymore since Gregory moved him to another dorm. In some ways, I miss him, and I'm sorry I lost his money. "If I tell you the truth, will you keep it under your hat?"

"Sure. Rumors have been flying since the morning old Collie found you'd gone over the wall. Hearing your side will be interesting."

"A nasty dude who wanted to sell me to his friend was dangling me by my ankle from a second story window and it fell out of my pocket. I got away from him, but when I went back later that night, the money was gone. So I guess he found it."

Jerry looks at me like he wants to take a ball bat to my head. Then he laughs. "What the hell. Keep it. That's a good story. Not worth a hundred bucks, but a good story."

I don't remind him it was more than a hundred bucks, or try to convince him that's what happened. I'm just glad Gregory has tamed him so he doesn't dare break any more of my bones.

"Next time," he stands up, "you can tell me about how you were driving the car and wrecked it trying to miss a little old lady crossing the street."

I fill days with board games, reading, watching educational videos, and wondering when my surprise package will arrive. Most nights I sleep through without dreams or interruptions, and without pills. Gregory keeps me on the sidelines because of my injuries, but they don't bother me much, and I walk around the track every morning and evening.

Even so, I'm restless. Start to call Ernie a few times, decide to wait and thank him after I know what the surprise is. Has John gone home to his farmhouse? We never learned what he did for a living, but with his secret bank account he's probably taking time off. Camping. Fishing. Driving his Caddy without worrying about cops. Wish I was with him.

The morning of the Fourth, I'm in my room, adding finishing touches to a rocket. If the timer works the way it should, and the launch doesn't fail, it's supposed to explode in the air and rain down in pieces like a puzzle that can be put back together.

An announcement over the intercom reminds us of a special presentation by a guest speaker, and the hubbub in the hall draws me out into the crowd.

We cross the lawn to the auditorium and file into seats reserved for us Middles. Somewhere behind us, a piece of hard candy arcs over our heads and into the Littles up front. Hits one, who swirls out of his seat like an angry cat to look for his attacker.

"Gotta be Jerry," Eric says beside me.

"I don't think so," I answer, and then I'm dumbstruck.

A slender young man is ushered onto stage by a junior dorm master who introduces him as Gordon Thomas, who has just flown into town from his university, and explains that the program is a slide show on saving the environment.

His neck hair has been trimmed so he looks scholarly, but the rest is long enough to cover the shaved spot where the sterile pad protected his scalp, skinned off on the rear view mirror. He's wearing wire-rimmed half glasses which I suspect are from a drug store rack, a long-sleeved white shirt and preppy pants like the ones he ruined washing in the rest area sink. Loafers with socks.

So this is my surprise. It's all I can do not to yell, Yea! Ernie! But I hold it in, knowing something's afoot and I don't want to spoil whatever he has in mind.

Organized, methodical, confident, he points to the pictures on the screen, and his voice is clear and authoritative. The program lasts about twenty minutes, the attention span of the Littles (and most Middles). When he shows the last slide— 'The End' — everybody starts clapping.

The junior dorm master marches from behind the curtain, and the applause freshens, mainly because, even geared for Littles, the show's the most excitement we've had all week and it's not time yet for the cook out. Nobody stands, we learned long ago to wait for permission. It's a good thing, as the JDM leans into the mic. "Our guest has asked for one of our Middles to give him the Grand Tour of the campus."

My hand shoots into the air, its plastic pinky guard unmistakable, seconds before other hands join it, some waving for attention. Ernie's bespectacled eyes rivet on me, and he speaks to JDM, who sounds like Bob Barker when he says, "Come on down! Binnie Scott, lucky Middle."

Sounds of laughter and jeering fade behind me as I make my way to the stairs leading onstage. JDM dismisses the audience and Ernie says with a straight face, "Hello, Binnie. I'm doing research on benevolent institutions such as East Wind, and I'd like to experience the rest of your day with you."

JDM is hovering, listening, so I answer in the same mode, "Mister Thomas, I'm honored to be your guide. Would you like to see my dorm, and the rocket I'm building for the celebration later tonight?"

"Fireworks, is it?" he asks, as we head in the direction of the dorms.

"You're leaving your slides," I remind him, but he carelessly says, "I'll pack them up later."

Steve's in the room when we get there, though after a formal introduction that strains my acting skills, he reluctantly departs for an appointment with his clarinet tutor.

I manage to close the door before we burst into laughter. "You dog! Why didn't you just tell me you were coming for a visit?"

"This was more fun, wasn't it? And I am doing research, for my major."

Typical Ernie. Writing papers before he has to. I show him the rocket, and he says, "Got any airplane paint?"

We filch some from the art department, along with small brushes, and he paints the word 'GOODBYE' on the nose cone. I like that, so we paint 'GOODBYE' on most of the puzzle-joined pieces, and I hope they don't burn too much to be read once they hit the ground.

"So what's been happening with you, Vinnie?"

"Other than skull-busting boredom?" I wipe off a smear of paint that went astray. "Found out my mom's alive and knows where I am. Has known since Day One."

"That's gotta hurt. I found out Fran's only my half sister. She's Dad's kid, but not Mom's. Which explains why Mom designated the trust fund just for me."

We're silent for a while, painting.

There's more. "When Francine went wild, I thought it was because of the money, but that was less than half of it. She found her birth certificate, right before she met Hoodoo. She was furious with Dad for starting the whole fiasco, with Mom because she let her think she was her real mother who just up and left her without any explanation."

He's not through yet. Clearing the air seems to help, so I just listen. "Dad has always been a private person, but what I didn't know was how his guilt had made him abuse Mom. That was why she left."

No wonder her sweet face looks sad. I want to say how sorry I am, but another silence falls and we leave it at that. When the rocket's covered with as many good bye's as we can fit on, all sizes and in red, white, and blue on the gun metal gray body, I set it in the window to dry.

"I brought transcripts from John's hearing." He pulls several tri-folded papers from his slacks pocket and we read each other's responses to the judge's questions. I'm impressed by the shrewdness of my companions, especially this part:

Judge: You admit to shooting Jordan.

John: I didn't shoot him for killing my wife. Had no proof of that. I shot him because he broke into my house.

There's a copy of Jordan's confession, which Ernie assures me was not coerced. The weapon wasn't an ax handle, the way Cuz Martin or Reporter Bob—I don't know which—claimed that day when I heard them in the coffee shop. It was a baseball bat

Margie kept beside her door in case of an intruder. Whether the crime was murder or manslaughter will be decided at Jordan's trial. His story, which must have been hard to tell, if true, is that Margie was planning to leave him. And take her money with her.

The report from Hoodoo's hearing explains how he'd found out from Francine about the case file Ernie was keeping, and the antique car, and it was easy for him to gain access to the grounds, with her key numbers.

Ernie clears up Hoodoo's motive for wanting to kill or at least maim her half brother. "Sufficient is never enough for people like Hoodoo, they have to go all out. Sabotaging my car was his way of getting even with me, not only for all the things he imagines I've done to him, but for who I am."

I lay the papers aside. "Do you know where John is now?"

"He went to the farmhouse."

I never did get my hands on a map, so I'm still confused about how far that might be from here. When I ask Ernie, he's already changing the subject.

"If you had to choose, what in this room would you save in case of a fire?"

I point to a handful of books. "Those."

"That's all?"

"Unless you brought my camera and running shoes. HEY! What about the photos? I thought you'd mail them to me and that would be your surprise."

He hands me an envelope of prints from his shirt pocket. There he is, leaning on John's Caddy in the parking lot. The three of us at lunch. At the tennis courts. And there's the old guy at the flea market who sold me the shoes. And, on the bottom, the first shot I took. Hoodoo's fist connecting with Ernie's jaw.

Out of the blue, I remember something else I would save, in case of fire. I haven't touched or even seen it since Collins shoved the box to the back of my closet shelf, the night I arrived at East Wind. We were both a lot younger then. And I'm still not tall enough to get the box down without Ernie's help.

171

Rabbit. He's about ten inches long, yellow fuzzy cloth, with beady eyes and nose, ears with wires that make them adjustable. The head and body are stuffed with something, but not the thin limp arms and legs. You'd expect a typical powderpuff bunny tail, but it's just a bit of cloth like the rest of him. Magnets for hands and feet so he hangs on stuff. Before I can cry over leaving him alone all these years, Ernie asks,

"What else have you got in there?"

Clothes to fit a five-year-old. A Christmas tree ornament with my name on it: Scott. A hand-tooled leather billfold, kid size. Opening it, I find a black and white photo of a woman and man under the protective plastic. My throat tightens. It's them, I want to say, but can't. Ernie's hand briefly touches my shoulder.

"You'll want to get to know her, one day."

"Yeah, probably."

We don't mention my dad, but if he's alive, I'll want to know that too. One day. Not soon. I fasten Rabbit's magnets around my arm, stuff him in my sling, and slip the wallet into my shorts pocket. "I travel light," I joke.

After some thought, I muse: "So I am Scott. Scott Vincent." I won't have to legally change my name. It's already the way I always wanted it.

"Whoever filled out your admission form must have left out the comma separating the first and last names, and they got switched."

"Remember when we were in the barracks at Haw Creek? I told you we were alike because we always want to do the right thing. We're alike another way, too. We have names that work both ways."

He smiles. "Comes in handy whenever you need an alias."

Steve returns from his lesson and we decide to show 'Mister Thomas' the rest of the campus. By the time we've finished touring the classrooms, gym, and library, there's a smell of lit charcoal in the air, and tables are loaded with uncooked hot dogs and burgers, packs of buns, containers of mustard and ketchup, covered bowls full of coleslaw, and coolers full of ice and drinks.

During the picnic, I try not to think of the last time we did this, a month ago, and the adventures I've had since Margie's lifeless body imprinted on my brain.

Ernie disappears for fifteen or twenty minutes, and I hope he hasn't taken off without saying— Goodbye.

He hasn't. He's on hand for chocolate brownies, and while most of the inmates compromise their digestion with baseball or soccer, he pulls my Scrabble board out of a canvas bag he's carrying around, along with my duffel. Nobody in the dorm will play me anymore, since I stopped throwing a game now and then. Ernie beats me two out of three.

Something else is in the bag. "Thought you might need them."

I pull on a thin pair of summer socks and slide my feet into my running shoes. They make me want to take them for a spin around the track, but that last hot dog persuades me otherwise.

Dusk comes early because of clouds rolling in, and it's a moonless night, so the fireworks start early in case it rains. Ernie remarks, "Shades of the festival."

"Too bad John can't be here."

If he answers, I don't hear him for the first volley. Ours aren't extravagant, but the show usually lasts maybe thirty minutes, with pauses between sets. We've watched maybe half when he says, "Ready for rocket launch? I brought it."

"Now? Sure."

I'd planned to climb the stairs to the walkway outside the library tower, and send Goodbye sailing toward the main buildings and picnic area. We do that together.

Forgot to bring matches. Ernie hasn't. "Boy Scout," I tease. I light the fuse and we stand back. The rocket sputters, teeters, smokes, then takes off . . . like a rocket.

We lean on the balcony railing and watch it arc over the gym and explode above the picnic grounds. I think about the debris left from the grill-out and figure all of it, including my rocket, will be raked up in the morning by old Martin before I'm even awake.

"I have one more surprise for you, Mouse."

Descending the steps in the dark, I'm thinking about what else he's been plotting. He's tossed away the empty canvas bag but is still carrying my duffel, which bulges. Probably stuffed with his slides.

Does this trek across campus mean he didn't arrive in a cab? Is a private small plane concealed somewhere beyond the garden plots, where he's leading me between rows of beans and squash? Before I can express doubt about whether he can safely navigate at night, we come to the farthest corner of the chain link fence, a good half mile from the fateful abandoned well, so no ghosts rise up to howl a lament.

The two-lane runs past here, darkly bordered by forest on both sides. I've never been in this direction, and excitement builds.

Ernie kneels about three feet out from the corner post, and shoves the duffel bag under the fence. Under the fence?

"Come on, Mouse. You're next." He guides me into a recently-shoveled ditch covered in painter's plastic. "I knew you'd never be able to climb with a broken collarbone."

"And pinky," I remind him, though truthfully I usually forget about it. "Why are we doing this?"

'Doing this' is sliding under the fence on my back, kicking out of his way as he follows me. We stand up, and I notice the distant street lamps. Wisps of fireworks smoke and an occasional illegal firecracker marks the end of the Fourth celebration.

He folds the plastic into a square convenient for carrying away.

"Look." He turns me around, picks up the duffel, and we start walking along the grassy shoulder of the road. What does he want me to see? In the starlight, between clouds, a shape moves towards us. It's a big, heavy car-shape, under blackout, easing over the tarmac in reverse. Stops about ten feet away. We run towards it.

Someone forgot to remove the dome bulb, because when Ernie opens the driver's side rear door and we pile in, by its light

I see John grinning, his arm over the seat. Next to him, Ernie's mom smiles at us.

The door closes and the light dies. John changes the gears to 'go' mode. "Well, Scott," she says, "are you ready for another life?"

Stunned but thrilled, I tell her, "I've been ready."

As the Caddy picks up speed on the straight, dark road, I'm torn between insane tears of joy and the urge to laugh out loud. Possibilities rush at me like fireworks, colorful and noisy. "Where are we going?"

"First, to my place," John says.

"We need to cut and bleach your hair," Ernie explains. He takes the drug store glasses from his pocket and fits them onto my face. No magnification. They're just a prop.

"And we can start home schooling right away, if you want," his mom adds. "Don't want you getting bored."

We round a curve and John clicks on the Caddy's lights. East Wind is history, hidden now by trees. Collins left without revealing any more about my real mother, but when the time comes, I'm sure I'll find her. Will she be sad in the meantime, not knowing where I am?

Ernie suggests, "Why don't you put Rabbit in the duffel with your books?"

As I do that, I remember the wallet in my pocket, and the photo in the wallet. Later at the farmhouse, I'll check to see whether anybody wrote my parents' names and maybe a date on the back.

"So how long have you guys known each other," I ask Ernie's mom. I've never heard her first name, and Mrs. Gordon makes her sound old and frumpy.

"We just met," she tells me. "Apparently we're almost neighbors."

Their smiles tell me there's a possible future there. I try to remember if Ernie ever said his parents are divorced or only separated. She's been out of the house for two years, so either way she's not likely to go back.

Ernie's looking smug. I sense there's some other shared secret that I don't know. Yet. My racing thoughts light on an entirely different matter. "Can we have banana pancakes for breakfast?"

"Sure," Ernie's mom says.

"And coffee?"

John and Ernie laugh. "Just don't let the kid make it," John advises.

"Why not?" She glances from one to the other, curious.

Ernie explains, "Oh, he can make it. If you like it strong."

"Strong enough to float an iron wedge," John warns her.

Mom's voice is calm, contented. "I like my coffee strong."

"Me, too," I tell them.

The two-lane stretches ahead, smoothly winding away behind us under the Caddy's wheels. I wonder how I'll look as a blond.

The End

www.ingramcontent.com/pod-product-compliance
Lightning Source LLC
Chambersburg PA
CBHW071601200626
46811CB00027BA/863